"Evocative . . . Nam as it
—Ed

"Vietnam: Ground Zero . . . are books to linger in the
mind long after their reading."
—*The Midwest Book Review*

After a few minutes Fetterman halted

"They stayed here quite a while," he whispered. He pointed to the spots where the vegetation was crushed and the jungle carpet disturbed. "Not much evidence, but enough."

Gerber glanced up at the canopy, but couldn't see the sky. "About seven hours to sunset."

Fetterman started off again. He skirted the huge trunk of a teak tree, then slipped between two palms. He walked slowly, eyes to the ground, the trees, then the canopy. He now knew that he only had to follow a compass course. The other squad hadn't varied from a straight path once they had left the LZ. Now he could look for signs that they had been followed. But the indication was that no one else had been in there for at least two weeks. The jungle quickly hid any signs.

For two hours they continued on, stopping and starting. Finally Fetterman called a halt. He waved Gerber forward.

"What's the problem?"

"We're there," Fetterman stated flatly.

"How do you know?"

"Captain, can't you smell it? We've found the missing men."

VIETNAM: GROUND ZERO™

MACV

ERIC HELM

A GOLD EAGLE BOOK FROM

WORLDWIDE®

TORONTO • NEW YORK • LONDON • PARIS
AMSTERDAM • STOCKHOLM • HAMBURG
ATHENS • MILAN • TOKYO • SYDNEY

First edition August 1989

ISBN 0-373-62719-X

VIETNAM: GROUND ZERO™
MACV

PROLOGUE

The young man in the dirty blue jeans and the ragged, faded work shirt moved among the knot of students, handing out rocks. He was bearded, with long brown hair clumped together by dirt and tied in a ponytail with a leather thong. He carried a rucksack filled with rocks, chunks of concrete and broken brick. Without approaching anyone from the front, he moved up behind them, slipped a stone into a hand and then moved on until he emptied his bag. Finished, he eased his way toward the rear of the crowd so that he could watch the confrontation.

A rank of police, dressed in dark blue uniforms and wearing white crash helmets, advanced across the open park, shoulder to shoulder. They held shields to protect their legs, stomachs and chests. As they entered the park, stomping the small bushes and flower beds flat, they stopped.

A police sergeant, moving behind his charges, raised a bullhorn to his mouth. "This is an unlawful assembly. You are requested to disperse immediately."

"Bullshit! Bullshit! Bullshit!" chanted the crowd in response.

"This an unlawful assembly," repeated the police officer. "If you do not peacefully disperse, you will be placed under arrest."

The crowd seemed to surge forward, and the man in the dirty clothes grinned. The cry of "Bullshit!" rang out again, almost drowning out the amplified voice of the police officer.

But neither side was moving far. The police had blocked the end of the park and now stood in the shadow of the trees, protecting the business district. They were content to remain there. The students, a surging, milling crowd of foul-mouthed children defying authority for the first time, were happy with the situation.

And then the first rock arced its way over the top of the crowd to slam into the police lines. It bounced from the gleaming shield and fell to the dirt of a ruined flower bed. For a moment nothing happened. It was as if both sides were surprised by the rock. A couple of police officers took unconscious steps to the rear and the line shrank toward the center.

There was a scream from a student as he ran forward, putting his body behind the throw. His stone hit another shield and bounced off.

"You are under arrest," yelled the sergeant with the bullhorn.

But before anyone could move, the student whirled and disappeared into the crowd, which opened ranks, let him in and reformed the line to protect him.

The police phalanx surged forward, pushing deeper into the park, moving around a huge tree and over picnic tables. The students began to scream. Rocks filled the air. A policeman was struck on the shoulder and slipped. Another tripped, falling to his knees. That seemed to spark the crowd. They edged forward toward the police line.

"You are ordered to disperse," shouted the sergeant with the bullhorn. He repeated the message over and over.

Behind him the streets were filled with police sirens as more officers rushed to the scene of the growing riot. Open ground, now littered with rocks and bottles, separated the two groups, but the gap between them was getting smaller. The uneasy peace had been shattered by the first rock. Now each side wanted to hurt the other, and the police officers forgot their first duty—to maintain order.

The man in the dirty clothes moved among the crowd, urging them to throw their rocks. "Come on, don't let the pigs push you around. This is a free country. You have the right to assemble. They're trying to suspend the Bill of Rights. Next you'll find yourselves in a rice paddy in Vietnam."

"Yeah," yelled a young man. "Hell no, we won't go."

"You will disperse now!" ordered the police sergeant.

"Facist!"

"Pig!"

"Asshole!"

The two sides then came together with an audible sound like that of breakers against a seawall. There was a wail, but not from police sirens. Students, young men and women, pushed against the police barricade of gleaming shields. Officers fell back, stumbled. Rocks hit their heads, bouncing off the shiny white helmets. An officer turned his head as a stone hit, cutting him badly. Blood stained his uniform.

At a signal from the sergeant, the police reacted with force, using their nightsticks on the crowd, swinging indiscriminately. A long-haired girl screamed and fell, her face bloodied. A police officer had his shield jerked from his hands. He punched with his fist, missed and stumbled. One protester jerked at his helmet and another hit him with a rock.

In the rear, the man in dirty clothes began gathering rocks and handing them to those around him. "Hit the pigs. Hit the pigs."

"You will disperse or be arrested," screamed the officer with the bullhorn.

As the police pushed past the wounded, three officers in regular uniforms and soft caps moved in, handcuffing the students caught behind the line. Those who offered any resistance were beaten.

The riot was in full swing now. Police officers waved their clubs, beating bloodied and arrested students into submission. The man in the dirty clothes eased his way to the rear of the crowd. He climbed a slight incline and looked down on the scene. A news photographer stood fifty yards away, taking pictures of the riot, and a film crew scrambled to get into position to shoot as the police pushed the students into the open. The filmmakers backed into a softball diamond and crushed the fence around the outfield.

"Yeah," said the man. He turned and ran down the hill and out of the park. He moved along the narrow street and up a hill toward an old brick building. He stopped for a moment and listened. More police sirens came, and he could hear noise from the swelling and echoing riot.

He opened the door that had long ago been painted blue. The paint was blistered and peeling. The man entered and moved down the dimly lighted hallway that smelled of mildew, vomit and urine, to a set of steps. He descended, entered another corridor that was darker than the one above it. The tile on the floor might once have been light gray, but was now dark, dirty and stained.

When the instigator came to another door, he used a key to open it. The lock was bright and new and would have resisted defeat if it had been necessary to break into the office.

As he stepped inside, another man looked up. "How'd it go?"

The room was brightly lighted, fluorescent tubes glowing overhead. There were three windows in one wall, but those had been covered with newspapers, and little sunlight penetrated. Along another wall were three four-drawer file cabinets, with a desk next to them. A kitchen table with five unmatched chairs stood opposite the desk. Two chairs had a floral design and might have belonged to the table, while the other three were metal folding chairs, one stenciled with YMCA. A camping table sat in the center of the room, set up as a conference table and surrounded by more stolen chairs. A green curtain partitioning one side of the room stood open, revealing a cot with a blanket and a mimeograph machine.

The dirty man sat on a folding chair and wiped the sweat from his face. He reached over the camp table and picked up a bottle of Coke, then drank deeply and replied, "Couldn't have gone better, Thom. Police overreacted and then the students went berserk. Going to be hundreds injured before it's all over."

Thom, a young man in faded blue jeans and a sweatshirt from the University of Colorado, sat down and leaned back, lacing his fingers behind his head. His hair was long, but trimmed and washed, and he was clean shaven.

"Got the riot going, then?"

"Wasn't hard." The disheveled man nodded. "I just hand out the rocks. Give someone a rock and he's going to throw it. Rocks hit the police and they're going to retaliate. Simple. Almost too simple. Maddening in that respect."

"Well, that's something, anyway."

"Not a hell of a lot, Thom. This really is too simple. News cameras there to record the event and all the dummies sit in their homes shaking their heads and asking themselves just what the hell this country is coming to."

"We're doing fine."

"We're not doing enough." The man got up and paced, touched a stack of fliers sitting on the table that listed American atrocities in Vietnam—the bombing of hospitals and the destruction of schools. He knew they were lies put out by Hanoi, but that made no difference. There were sources available, and to many that meant they were the truth.

"What more can we do? We alert the people to the war in Vietnam, turn their opinion against it. We help stage rallies, putting people in the street. The Students for a Safe Society are out in force raising money."

"Kids' games. It's all kids' games. We're not accomplishing much of anything here. Some news footage that isn't going to sway opinion, except to convince people that the students should all be locked up." He moved around the table and looked up at the newspaper-covered windows as if he could see through them into the street.

"Social change moves slowly."

"But war changes things overnight."

Thom shrugged. "It's the way of the world."

"Those riots—" he turned to face Thom and pointed "—aren't the answer. All we're doing is spinning our wheels. People are getting hurt out there."

"Not seriously. Students aren't being killed. A little violence, a little trauma, is good for the soul."

"Says who?"

"Now who's playing the kids' games."

The man sat down again and leaned forward, elbows on the table. "It's not enough. We're not making a significant change. If I thought we were, maybe I could work up a little more enthusiasm for our task."

"That's all we can do. Inform the people. Let them know what's happening in Southeast Asia. Convince them we have to act together to get our soldiers out of Asia."

"No. Sitting here and writing our pamphlets and stories is not the answer."

"These were the things that fired the American Revolution," Thom replied. "Men discussing ideas and ways of resisting those ideas. Civil disobedience to convince our leaders that we have opinions. Political action. Voting out the candidates who keep American soldiers in Vietnam, and voting in those who are opposed to the war.''

The man laughed. ''That's not the way social change is accomplished. It's done by brave men with vision who have the courage to put their plans into play. Sitting on the sidelines just isn't the answer.''

Thom stood and moved to the table where the Coke sat. After emptying the bottle he said, ''You did a nice job on the sidelines today.''

''You don't understand.''

''I understand perfectly,'' Thom said. ''Social change is accomplished by men of vision who can manipulate the media and public sentiment to their cause.''

''No. Social change is accomplished by men who act decisively. We're leaving the change up to others. All we're doing is acting as catalysts. We make a move in one direction and hope that a change is initiated in another direction. That's just not the way it's done.''

''I know you,'' Thom said. ''You've got something in mind now.''

''Yes, I do.'' He grinned. ''But you're not going to like it. First, I must shed this image. Cut my hair and shave. Clean up my act.''

''And give up all the free pussy you've been getting. Those college bimbos are only too willing to peel out of their clothes and spread their legs for you.''

''Some things transcend the easy sex.''

''I think you're beginning to talk heresy. No college man would say that.''

''I'm serious here.''

''So am I.''

''Thom, I want you to understand that I haven't abandoned our cause, our beliefs. It's just that I don't think what we're doing here is going to accomplish our goals. I've got to do something more than hand out rocks to start riots.''

"You're quitting. That's what you're saying."

"I'm afraid so. I have an idea that might advance our cause faster than anything we could ever hope to do here. A plan that should be easy to implement, one that has a real chance of working. Power, real power, isn't in the hands of the poor students."

Thom shook his head. "I've heard all this before. It sounds exactly like the speech made by the man who is about to sell out."

"And it's going to look that way. I've got to get myself settled into the power structure. Once I've found a good position, I'll be better able to effect the changes we want."

"All right. I believe you. All I can do is wish you the best of luck."

"And with it, you'll hear from me again."

The two men shook hands. As Thom stood there in the center of the tiny office-apartment, his comrade turned and left, never to return. But Thom would hear from him again.

1

The resident agent of the Central Intelligence Agency, Jerry Maxwell, stood at the head of the table in the small conference room and wished he could get the hell out. The room was hot and seemed to be closing in on him. The walls, made of plywood and painted light green, were not restful. They made him sick. The conference table, an old wooden thing that might once have been expensive, was warped by the humidity, stained by too many glasses left sitting on it for too long and discolored by the years in the tropics. But it was good enough for its purpose.

Maxwell was a short, slender man who dressed in wrinkled and stained white suits, white shirts, and normally wore a skinny black tie, loosened. He had dark hair and eyes and, after nearly two years in Saigon, had finally acquired a tan. He had lost his perpetual sunburn, though his nose was still red.

Pulling a handkerchief from his back pocket, he wiped the sweat from his face. It was so hot in the room that his hair was soaked and his armpits damp. He moved to a small podium that stood in one corner, and glanced at the screen across the room. His new assistant sat behind the slide projector, running it by hand since someone had recently lost the remote control device.

"All right, Sergeant," said Maxwell, "we have a photo here of the market area of Kampong Trach, which is maybe twelve klicks over the border in Cambodia."

Army Staff Sergeant Perry Kinson sat at the conference table. He wore clean jungle fatigues, but they were old, faded to gray-green. His stripes, name tag and U.S. Army tag were all in black thread. The pockets were all buttoned, his jungle boots were shined, and although his uniform wasn't starched, it had been pressed. His sandy-colored hair was cropped short, with white side walls. Light blue eyes made him look older than he was. A young man, he had shaved closely just before the meeting, had fine features, small ears and a long nose. Like Maxwell he was deeply tanned, but whereas Maxwell seemed almost fleshy from the massive Saigon meals, Kinson was gaunt. C-rations and meals at the fire-support bases did that. If someone could have thought of a way to export the stuff to the World for weight-loss clinics, he would have been rich.

Kinson shifted uneasily in his chair, glanced at the unidentified civilian running the projector and said, "Cross-border operations are . . ."

"Run everyday," Maxwell finished. "Granted, they're covert, but we've got to keep track of what the enemy is doing across the border. Rumors about their operations must be checked and double-checked."

"Yes, sir."

Maxwell nodded and the picture changed, showing a map of the region. "As you can see, there's some swampy area both north and south of the target zone, but the region itself is moderate to heavy jungle. Plenty of cover for you. Not much of a hike into Cambodia."

Kinson rubbed a hand over his chin. "I don't understand why you're using the regular Army for this."

Maxwell took a deep breath and exhaled audibly. "Sergeant, there are only so many resources available here. You happen to be one of them."

"Yes, sir," said Kinson. "I understand that. What I'm worried about is this cross-border operation. We've been told over and over that we're not to cross into Cambodia. It's neutral territory. Period."

"Sergeant," Maxwell responded, "I can provide you with written orders detailing your responsibilities. Although it won't spell out the mission across the border, it will state that you are to obey my instructions."

"Yes, sir," Kinson agreed. "I just wanted to be clear on that point."

"Now, if I may continue." He glanced at the Army man and then at his assistant.

"Yes, sir." Kinson nodded.

Maxwell mopped his face again and moved to the map. He explained what he had in mind, detailing the operation from the moment Kinson and his men piled out of the choppers until they returned to Saigon. They were to make no contact with the enemy. They were to avoid a confrontation under all circumstances, running instead of fighting. Theirs was a sneak-and-peek operation. Check on the North Vietnamese in town, then get out. Maxwell wanted to know how many enemy soldiers were there and what they were doing. Just a count. Weapons, men, vehicles, everything of a military nature. After two or three days they were to sneak back into South Vietnam and be picked up by helicopters.

The briefing was illustrated with slides of the territory showing that the jungle wasn't as dense as some. Part of it was triple canopy, part of it double. The ground was overgrown but not with the almost impenetrable barriers of vegetation found in the central highlands. It was a simple recon that shouldn't last more than five days. Easy.

"How do I tell the North Vietnamese from the Cambodes?" Kinson asked.

"You'll be provided with two Cambodian scouts. Ethnically the Cambodes are shorter and darker than the North Vietnamese. You'll be able to tell them apart. You know how to tell the soldiers."

Kinson reached up and brushed his fingers against his short hair. "NVA favor the buzz cuts."

"They'll be better fed than the civilians. More robust. They'll have big shoulders and big chests from carrying those packs. They'll be young men, and the Cambodians will probably stay clear of them."

"Yes, sir."

Maxwell left the podium and sat down at the table. He looked at his assistant. "You can shut off the projector and head down to the office to wait."

"Sure." The civilian hurried out of the room.

As he stood to leave, Maxwell said, "Remember, this is a sneak-and-peek operation. You, five or six men and the two scouts. In and out."

"Yes, sir."

"You have any questions?"

"When do we jump off?"

"Tomorrow morning. You'll catch the choppers over at Hotel Three, refuel at Tay Ninh and hit the field about midmorning. I'd suggest you move toward the border but not cross until dark. By the following morning you should be close to the target. Lie low and observe. Stay two days minimum. Then, if you feel you have everything you need, pull out."

"Yes, sir." Kinson hesitated. "Can I ask why we're doing this?"

"Certainly, but I don't want to hear anything about it coming back to this office. Keep your mouth shut."

"Yes, sir."

Maxwell leaned forward. "Indications are that the enemy is going to try another push toward Saigon. He had some success the first time during Tet. Not much, but some. More importantly, he got a lot of press about the VC running through the streets. Now he's going to try to engineer something like that again. Something that will look good on the evening news. We want to prevent that from happening. Your team will help us get a handle on the size of the force being mounted."

Kinson nodded. "I understand, sir."

"Fine. If you'll return here about fifteen hundred hours, you'll have a chance to meet with the Cambodian scouts, get your radio codes and your escape-and-evasion codes, and be briefed on the latest intel."

"They'll be here? The Cambodians?"

"Yes. We want to get everyone introduced to everyone else. We figured it'd be a good idea to have you see one another before the mission."

"And the rest of the squad? Who chooses them?"

"You pick who you want on your team. Five or six. I don't want a fucking parade into Cambodia. Take a look and get out. Report back to me. You don't tell anyone else anything until you've talked to me."

"Yes, sir." Kinson headed toward the door.

"Sergeant," Maxwell said, trying to make his voice hard, to add a look of hostility to his eyes. "I don't want to hear about this mission from someone else, and I don't want to read about it in the papers."

"No problem."

CAPTAIN MACKENZIE K. GERBER sat in the rear of the cab and tried not to think about the odors that were blowing up into his face. There seemed to be a hole somewhere in the floorboards, and the air blew in, swirled around under the seat and then hit him full in the face. An evil, rotten odor, like heated vomit and warmed urine. He turned and rolled the window the rest of the way down and stuck his face out. The smell of Saigon wasn't much better.

Gerber was a Special Forces officer now assigned to MACV-SOG, which the press thought meant Studies and Observations but which actually meant Special Operations Group. He was a young man, just thirty years old, tall and slim. He had brown hair and light-colored eyes that were sometimes blue and sometimes steel gray. Deeply tanned from his time in Vietnam, he was strong—and just a little annoyed. The smell from the cab was beginning to get to him.

Squeezed in the back between him and Sergeant Anthony B. Fetterman, was Robin Morrow, a reporter who had more time in-country than any two combat officers either of them would care to name. Only a few of the oldest Special Forces NCOs and officers could match her.

She was tall and slender, now almost gaunt. The pressures of Vietnam, of her recent trip into Cambodia and the trouble she'd had getting back to Saigon, were telling on her. There were dark circles under her green eyes and lines on her face that hadn't been there six months earlier. Her light brown hair was bleached blond by the tropical sun. An intelligent woman, she actually understood the Special Forces and their role in the war. She wasn't the type of journalist to sit around Saigon, talk about how rough it was, then have another drink. She got into the field, talked to the men—the enlisted men—and learned exactly what was happening. She was fooled by neither the brass hats at MACV nor the other reporters in the news bureau.

Master Sergeant Fetterman was a study in contrast. He was short, almost diminutive, and was balding on top but had a thick band of black hair. His beard was so heavy he had to shave twice a day or look as if he hadn't shaved during the past week. Like the others, he was heavily tanned, and that did tend to hide the dark growth on his chin and cheeks. He was nondescript until you looked into his eyes, which weren't blue and weren't brown. They were blue-black and cold, killer's eyes, and had a way of frightening people who didn't know him.

"You think this is a good idea?" asked Fetterman.

Gerber turned and looked at the master sergeant. "Hell, Tony, it seems to be a lousy one."

"I could have gotten us a jeep."

"Yes, but I thought a cab would be nicer," said Gerber.

"You shouldn't have taken the first one to dive out of traffic."

"We could always get out," Morrow said.

Gerber looked at her. Sweat was beaded on her upper lip and in her hairline. She wore a light dress, cut low. When she pulled the material away from her chest and blew down the front, she saw that both Gerber and Fetterman were watching her.

"Cools me off," she said with a grin.

"Has the opposite effect on me," said Gerber.

She looked down and realized that she was revealing more than she had intended to, and pushed her hand against her chest. "Oops."

"I should say so," said Fetterman.

Gerber turned his attention back to the streets. He inhaled deeply and nearly choked. A military truck in front of them belched a cloud of dense black smoke.

"That's all we need," he said.

"If you're going to complain all the way," Fetterman groaned, "let's get out and walk."

Gerber shook his head "no," and they continued down a couple of wide streets. Traffic was all around them, from the pedicabs holding one or two people to the Lambretta—a scooterlike vehicle with a pickup truck bed on the back to carry passengers—to cars and trucks, many of them military. Heavy traffic. Soldiers in the backs of the trucks shouted at the pedestrians, some of the comments off-color.

"I wish they wouldn't do that," Gerber muttered.

Fetterman shrugged. "Just letting off a little steam."

"I don't blame them," said Gerber, "but it gives a bad impression. Makes the Vietnamese think we're all like that. Big mouths with no class."

"If you'd been in the field for a month . . ."

"I said I understood it, Tony. I don't have to like it." His voice indicated the discussion was over.

"Yes, sir."

Morrow leaned closer to Fetterman, touched his sleeve and asked, "What's gotten into Mack?"

"I don't know," Fetterman replied. "He's been this way since we got back from the field. I thought maybe hanging around with you would improve his attitude."

"So did I, but all we've done is eat breakfast."

"If you two are finished discussing my mental state and my attitude—"

"No reason to get annoyed, Mack," interrupted Morrow.

"No, not at all," said Gerber sarcastically. "My two very good friends pretend that I'm not here."

Just then the taxi swerved, a horn blared and there was a squeal of tires.

"Jesus," snapped Gerber. He slapped the back of the seat. "Take it easy."

Ignoring the instruction, the driver glanced over his shoulder and grinned.

Morrow reached out and took Gerber's hand. "Mack?"

"Captain. It's not that important," said Fetterman quietly.

Gerber fell back in the seat and closed his eyes. He took a deep breath and then let it out slowly. "Sometimes it just gets to you. All the pressure, all the decisions, the constant strain. The noise and the smells and the godawful heat. You just want to get away, into a hot tub, and sleep the night without worrying about a mortar dropping on you. Sleep in a cool bed with air-conditioning."

"Maybe it's time to take some R and R," said Fetterman.

Gerber snorted. "We've only been here about six months."

"Then it's the right time for R and R. Maybe a little trip to Bangkok or Taipei or Singapore."

The taxi started forward, slipping into the flow of traffic, first following a truck and then sliding in behind a jeep. They swerved again, but this time it wasn't as violent.

"R and R is a good idea," said Gerber. "Robin, can you get away for a couple of days?"

She smiled. "You want to foot the bill? Take me to some exotic place?"

"Christ, you make more money than Tony and I put together. You should take us."

"I have to pay taxes," she said.

"Okay," said Gerber. "You have to pay taxes, but you're still making the big bucks. I think you should take us."

She turned serious. "I'm not sure I can get away right now. I've spent the past few weeks in Japan and I haven't gotten back into the swing of things here."

Gerber rubbed a hand over his face and then wiped it on the leg of his jungle fatigue pants. "Now's the perfect time for us. It's slow down here. Marines still fighting in the north, but it's quiet around here."

Morrow shrugged. "There isn't much going on here for us either. If I knew where you were going, I might be able to think of a way to get there."

"Then it's settled," said Fetterman. "We get to Tan Son Nhut, I'll slip over to the SOG building and see what's available."

"What do you mean, see what's available?" asked Morrow.

Fetterman turned toward her. "We've got quotas on the R and Rs. We can't decide to hit just any R and R center. There has to be space available on the flights. I'll see what's open and when we can get out."

"Doesn't seem fair," said Morrow.

"You want to hear something not fair," Gerber snorted. "I'll tell you something not fair. The headquarters pukes and the supply pukes get first choice because they're around when the quotas arrive. Sometimes you only get the leftovers. Nothing you can do unless you want to wait."

"Well," said Morrow, "I'm sure Tony will be able to work something out."

When they slowed for the front gate at Tan Son Nhut, the guard appeared, dressed in jungle fatigues, wearing a steel pot and flak jacket and carrying an M-16. Bending at the waist, he saw the Americans in the back seat and waved them through.

"I see security has slipped back into its old habits."

"You going to start again, Captain?" asked Fetterman.

"I was merely commenting that they seem to have forgotten the lessons of Tet quickly."

"Not your problem."

"No, Tony. Not my problem until they start coming through the wire at me, helped by all the people the gate guard let through."

Fetterman shook his head and rolled his eyes. "Robin, I think maybe you should take the Captain to the club and buy him a big drink. Maybe that'll settle him down."

Morrow laughed. "I don't think a drink is what he needs."

Fetterman was about to ask what it was he did need and then realized what she was saying. "Oh."

"Exactly," said Morrow. "Oh."

JERRY MAXWELL WAS SITTING in his office, his feet up on his desk, and reading a classified report. His desk, an old battleship-gray monstrosity that might have seen its first service during the Civil War, was stuck in the corner, awash with reports, documents, files and papers. One side was lined with empty Coke cans. Next to it was a single chair for visitors, a metal tube thing with vinyl cushions that had been repaired with black electrician's tape.

The walls were cinder block, painted the same sickening green color that had dominated the conference room. Framed prints of the local scene hid a crack in the wall and a spot that leaked water.

Opposite him was a bank of file cabinets. The one at the end, tucked in against the wall, was a massive thing with a combination lock on the center drawer. The tops of the cabinets held more papers and files.

There was a knock at the door. Maxwell turned, saw that his safe was closed and then yelled, "Come on in."

His assistant, a young man with short brown hair, a sunburned complexion and wide-set blue eyes, entered. He was a nervous man with quick, flighty movements. He couldn't sit still, often tapping the table with his fingers or shaking a foot as he sat. He had small hands and thin fingers. His mother had told him often that he would make a good brain surgeon. Philip Reed was short and thin, and he had spent the past four years in college, getting a degree in political science while drinking gallons of beer.

He entered and sat down in the visitor's chair without waiting for an invitation. He stared at Maxwell. "I've completed the report. I've got a good map of Kampong Trach and a couple of new aerial photos for them."

"You be ready at fifteen hundred to brief?"

"I believe I'll be able to handle it."

"Then there's no reason for me to hang around." Maxwell picked up a Coke can and shook it. It was empty.

Reed leaned back in the chair, his briefing folder in his lap. "Is this really a good idea?"

"Shit, you've been listening to that sergeant. What could go wrong? It's a sneak-and-peek operation. Put a couple of men into the field to look at the enemy's strength and location. A recon is all I want."

"Across the border. The sergeant was right about that. We're not supposed to be operating in Cambodia."

"What are you?" asked Maxwell. "The fucking *Washington Post*? Technically no one's supposed to be in Cambodia. Not our guys and not theirs. They have bases there and we need to take a look. No problem."

"I just thought I should say something about it. I mean, in the papers back in the World, everyone is pretending that we're fighting the war fairly."

Maxwell closed his folder and tossed it at the pile on his desk. He dropped his feet to the floor and looked at the young man sitting opposite him. "I'm about to fill you in on the way things are in the real world. There is what the newspapers report, there are the way things should be, and there are the way things are. The newspapers pretend that everyone honors the neutrality of Cambodia. They concede that the North Vietnamese might sometimes use trails through Cambodia to bring supplies into South Vietnam. The way things should be, there are no trails in Cambodia and no one—not us, not them, not the VC—ever ventures across the line."

He stopped talking and looked into the eyes of the young man sitting in the chair. "This getting through to you?"

"I thought we were the good guys. We played by the rules, even if the other side didn't."

"Son," said Maxwell, feeling older than his years, "that's what's known as growing up. You could stay back in the World, going to college forever, finding a teaching position and never learn what's really happening."

"Nothing wrong with a college education," Reed said indignantly.

"Did I miss something?" asked Maxwell. "Did I say there was anything wrong with college? No. I merely said that it was possible to stay in that environment and never have to enter the real world. You get out here and you have to grow up.

That's the difference between what's going on here and what's happening on the college campuses."

There were things that Reed wanted to say. He wanted to tell Maxwell that by coming down to the level of the enemy, we hurt ourselves more than we hurt him. He wanted to tell him that only honorable men should have high positions in the government. He wanted to tell Maxwell that someone had to have the ideals or the world would end up in a bucket of shit. Someone had to see the clear, righteous path and force the others to follow along it.

He wanted to say all that, but he knew Maxwell would never listen. His boss had been exposed to so much that he was a hard-core cynic. Nothing Reed could say would convince him that he needed to play by the rules. Maxwell believed in his heart that rules were made to be broken.

Instead Reed kept his opinions to himself and said, "I'll brief the sergeant."

"And when you do, make sure you check the ID of anyone he brings with him, or get him to vouch for anyone he brings. Sometimes the security managers try to slip in a ringer so that they can fault us on COMSEC. They want us to fuck up so they'll have a report to file."

"You're kidding. They pull that stuff here? In Vietnam?"

"Son, they'll pull it anywhere. You have to be ready for the games or you'll find yourself in the fucking latrine, scrubbing the toilets until they can ship your butt out of here."

"I'll be careful."

Maxwell picked up his report and then glanced at Reed. "You let me know just before you start the briefing. Maybe I'll sit in."

Reed, realizing he had been dismissed, stood. "Of course." He left without another word.

2

ENLISTED QUARTERS
TAN SON NHUT AIR BASE
SOUTH VIETNAM

Perry Kinson sat on his bunk and stared at the dirty plywood
floor. A box fan sat on a footlocker nearby, blowing muggy air
at him, but it did little to dry the sweat that soaked his OD
T-shirt. He glanced over at the sleeping form of Spec Four
William Hurtz. He wore only his underwear and OD socks.
Sweat covered his skinny frame, and beaded on his face. His
pillow showed dark stains where the perspiration had dripped
onto it. His face and arms were deeply tanned while the rest
of him was a pasty white.

Another man entered the barracks carrying a towel and
wearing shower shoes. He stood naked in the doorway and
said, "God, this is the life. Hot showers in the middle of the
day. Steaks at the club. We're doing something wrong. What
they're doing is punishing us by keeping us in the field all the
fucking time."

"Yeah," said Kinson.

Spec Four Sam Burgess was a big man, six foot odd and
weighing over two hundred pounds. Unlike his fellow soldiers he seemed to thrive on Army food. He loved the ham and

lima beans in the C-ration meals and was probably the only living American who could make that claim. He rubbed his dark hair with the towel and then grinned, showing perfect teeth. He wiped his face, closed his bright blue eyes and then opened them.

As he moved into the room, he asked, "You have a problem there, Sarge?"

Kinson looked up. "We've a briefing in about an hour. Over at MACV."

Burgess crossed the floor and tossed his towel onto his bunk. "Well, shit, that ruins my plans."

"Short briefing," added Kinson. "But then we'll be in the field tomorrow."

"Nope," said Burgess. "Just no fucking way. I've a date tonight. Little mamasan who won't be able to wait to get out of her clothes for me. None of this we've-got-a-patrol-in-the-morning shit."

Hurtz sat up then, blinking rapidly. He rubbed his head and asked, "What the fuck is all the noise?"

"The sergeant has announced that we've a briefing in about an hour."

"Why?" Hurtz sounded like a little kid wanting to know why he had to eat all his vegetables.

"Because we're here," said Kinson.

Burgess climbed into OD shorts and asked, "What's that mean?"

"It means that I need two or three guys to go with me and you two are here."

"If I hadn't come back from the shower, you'd have found someone else?"

"No, Sam. I'd have come looking for you. Anyway, we all get to go tomorrow. It's just that I'd like a couple of other guys at the briefing this afternoon. You'll still be able to make your date."

Burgess sat down on his cot, then leaned back, laced his hands under his head and stared up at the ceiling. There were canopies from parachute flares draped through the rafters. A fan spun slowly, whipping at the canopy, leaving a black streak on the silk.

"I'm not sure I want to go."

Kinson stood up and moved to where his fatigue shirt was hanging. "I'm not sure that I care what you want. You're going. So is Hurtz. And if anyone is dumb enough to walk through that door in the next twenty minutes, then he's going to get to go too."

Almost as if to answer a call from on high, Private First Class Nevelle Tideman walked in. He was dressed in civilian clothes, a flowered shirt in blues, greens and aquas. He wore khaki pants and black low quarters. Tideman was the real kid of the bunch, having turned eighteen a week before he got orders to Vietnam. He'd joined the Army at seventeen and a half with his parents' permission. They'd wanted him out of the house and didn't care that he might end up twelve thousand miles away. If there had been a way to get him to the moon, they'd have taken it. But he didn't mind being that far away from them, either. What he didn't know was that they were both back home bragging to anyone who'd listen about their brave son fighting in Vietnam.

A tall bony kid with long brown hair that touched his ears and had gotten him into trouble with more than one NCO, he didn't look like he'd have the strength to hump the boonies. He did have broad shoulders, but almost no waist. His face was long with the cheekbones showing through. He was trying to grow a mustache and failing at that.

"You too," said Kinson.

"Me too, what?" asked Tideman.

"Get into a uniform. We've a briefing to go to."

"Not me. I've got a date in a little while, and I'm not passing it up."

Kinson looked heavenward, as if searching for salvation. To Tideman he said, "I don't believe that was a request. It was an order. Get into a uniform, or you'll find yourself on point for the rest of your life, and the way you fuck up, that won't be for very long."

"Thanks a whole hell of a lot," snapped Tideman. He began to unbutton his shirt and then yanked on it, scattering the buttons. He tossed it at the wall locker. "Fuck it. Just fuck it."

Kinson ignored that. He turned and looked out at the air base. Men were walking along the neat streets. Several of them, in jungle fatigues, were working their way along, picking up cigarette butts and other trash while an NCO sat in the passenger's seat of a jeep watching them. He was smoking a cigar that looked like a huge stick of brown dynamite.

It was a strange war, Kinson decided. One day in the field, shooting at the enemy, and the next in Saigon, probably dancing with women who were also the enemy. Soldiers stuck in a war zone half a world from home, picking up cigarette butts so that the base would look neat. Sure as hell wouldn't want a messy base in case a general or a senator arrived on an inspection or a fact-finding tour.

Sitting down on his bunk, Kinson realized the reason for policing the area. Not that it would inhibit the fighting if the war suddenly came to them, but for the discipline it instilled. The value of cleaning the camp wasn't in the cleaning, but in the discipline. Pride in your unit could turn you into a fighting machine. Sloppy soldiers might not be bad soldiers, and the straightest soldiers might not be the best, but those with pride were hard to beat. They believed themselves invincible. They wanted their bases, their uniforms, their equipment to look sharp. They were ready for a parade or an enemy assault. It was a fine point that civilians just couldn't understand.

"We going to get transport over to this briefing?" asked Burgess.

"Over and back," said Kinson. "I've got a jeep arranged. We'll drive over."

"Long as we're back by seventeen hundred so I can make my date," said Burgess.

"I'll let the general know of your schedule so that we can plan accordingly."

"I appreciate it."

AT TAN SON NHUT, Fetterman let them off at the closest gate to the World's Largest PX. Then he drove off toward the SOG compound. Gerber watched the taxi disappear down the road and looked at Morrow.

"Anything you want to look at in the PX?"

"Nothing specific. I just want to look around."

They walked through the gate guarded by an AP wearing pressed jungle fatigues, a new flak jacket and a steel pot. He had a pistol in a holster and a new M-16. He saluted Gerber as they approached.

Inside the building was a large entrance area with lock boxes on one wall for weapons. Another AP stood inside the door to ensure that everyone complied with the regulations. Gerber wasn't carrying his rifle, and his Browning M-35 pistol was concealed under his jungle jacket. With Morrow he walked straight into the warehouselike area of the main PX. No one asked to see her ID card to ensure that she was authorized in the PX. They just figured all Americans were cleared.

"Never ceases to amaze me," said Gerber.

"What?"

He grinned and waved a hand. "We should let the enemy in here. Let him see everything that's available."

"You mean we'd be able to buy them."

Gerber shrugged. "I hadn't thought of it that way. I suppose we could buy some support. Hell, I guess we're doing it here in Saigon with all our allies, but no, I had something else in mind. I'd just let them in to look at this.''

''Why?''

''Make them think. They're out in the field and it's quite a task to get them the ammunition and equipment they need. They're required to steal food from the local population. They live a real hand-to-mouth existence, and if there's a major problem in their army, it's keeping the lines of communication open and the supplies flowing.''

''Okay,'' said Morrow, still not understanding.

''Then,'' said Gerber, ''I'd bring them in here.'' He entered the main area, dragging Morrow with him. He moved along a wall that was lined with magazines and books. Hundreds of them. He stopped in a corner and pointed. ''I'd show them this.''

Morrow looked up at the mannequin. A female dressed in a filmy negligee, bikini-type panties and a garter attached to dark stockings.

''Bribe them with women?''

''You being deliberately obtuse? No. Show them the might of the American Army by showing them just how much support our soldiers get. We don't have trouble getting the men ammo, equipment, food or anything else. In fact, we have such a method of resupply that we can waste it on shipping goods that have absolutely no military value.''

Morrow stared up at the display and then at the counter that held more of the same. Teddies, stockings, garters, lace panties. ''I see what you mean.''

''There's no way to defeat an army that spends so much to ship so little to the fighting men. It's not like they can use the stuff themselves.''

Now Morrow grinned. ''Oh, I don't know. Remember all the World War Two movies where the GI gives the French girl some stockings to earn her undying gratitude. The Vietnamese women should appreciate this stuff.''

"You know what I mean."

"Yes, I see that. If we have that kind of money, time and effort to waste, if we brought all that to bear on them, they wouldn't stand a chance."

"None. It'd be a real psychological victory for us. One they couldn't counter."

She moved closer to him. She bumped a warm hip against his and asked, "But ignoring the geopolitical implications of garters and stockings, is there anything there that you'd like to see modeled?" Her voice had dropped, taking on a husky, sexy quality.

"You sure know how to end a discussion quickly."

"Well, is there anything?"

"You find something light, filmy and see-through and I think I'd appreciate it just fine."

"Meaning what?"

"Meaning I'll leave you here to pick it out, and I'll go off to see what they have in the way of cameras and stereos."

"Okay."

Gerber left her standing there, looking at the lingerie. He moved through the aisles, seeing everything that the well-dressed soldier could need. Cameras, televisions, jewelry, stereos, fur coats, records, tapes, film, radios and a fully stocked grocery area. Boxes of detergent, food, cookies and cases upon cases of beer and Coke. More of it than any two stores in the world would need. More than he'd seen in one place. Ever.

He wandered around, wondering what he should buy. Without a permanent camp, he was afraid to buy anything that would have to be moved. At the hotel where he stayed while in Saigon, he could store a stereo, but the current in the hotel was different from that in the World. To take the stereo home when he DEROSed would mean that he'd have to have the stereo changed, or he'd have to sell it to someone just arriving.

He studied a couple of the units. They were unbelievably cheap. He could get everything, including a tape deck, for a couple of hundred bucks. He could probably sell the system easily when he went home. There were always a lot of young men with more money than they could spend, hanging around looking for a bargain from the men going home.

Morrow caught him and said, "You thinking of buying something?"

He hesitated and then shook his head. "I'm afraid it'd be more trouble than it's worth. Maybe a radio." He looked at her sack. It was tiny. "Hey, I like that, if your whole costume is in there."

"Everything I need is in this tiny little bag."

"Let me see."

"Oh no. You wouldn't help me pick it out, so I'm not going to let you look at it yet." She grinned devilishly. "So, you want to look at radios?"

Gerber scratched his head. Not far away was a stack of small black-and-white televisions for just over fifty dollars each. He edged in that direction.

"You're not going to buy a set are you?"

"Why not? Little TV after a hard day in the war. Maybe watch a little Carson or something. Besides, it's only fifty dollars."

She waved the sack under his nose. "Watch a little television, huh?"

"Not every night," said Gerber. "But there are times when you're not around and it feels good to veg out. Watch TV with the brain in neutral."

"Go ahead then. Buy one."

Gerber moved to the stack and looked them over. They were all small, the screens nine or ten inches, had rabbit ears and only a VHF dial. No UHF capability. Nothing too fancy, but then he wasn't in the World with a dozen different options.

He plucked a box from the stack and moved toward the counter where he could pay for it. They worked their way through the checkout area where the Vietnamese girls manned the cash registers and insisted they didn't speak English.

On their way out the door, they spotted Fetterman. Gerber moved toward him and asked, "You want to go in there?"

"No, Captain, I have all the fur coats I need." He spotted the box. "But you didn't."

"Just a television."

"Isn't that like saying she's just a little pregnant?"

"Now what's that supposed to mean?"

Fetterman looked at Morrow. "It starts small. First they're listening to the radio. Then it's only a show or two once a week on the TV. The next thing you know they're sitting in the dark, night after night, watching everything thrown at them, including the commercials."

"Jesus Christ in the television studio," said Gerber. "If I had known it was going to bother the two of you so much, I would have passed up the urge."

"It's like a drug," said Morrow, picking up the ball. "Not much at first, and then everything."

Gerber shook his head and looked at Fetterman. Trying to change the subject, he asked, "What'd you learn about the R and R situation?"

"Not real good now. Seems that everything has slowed down, so everyone and his brother are putting in for R and R. All the choice ones are taken, and there is a list a mile long for Australia."

"We've been there," said Gerber.

"Yes, sir. The point is, we could get to Bangkok in about three weeks, if we wanted to stay in a hot, tropical, Asian environment."

"Not what I had in mind," said Gerber.

"Hawaii is out," said Fetterman. "Married guys are getting all those."

"Then there isn't much available . . ."

"No, sir. They claimed that if we wanted to wait, he'd put our names on a list. They'd let us know when we could leave."

"And we'd be in the field, unable to return, and some asshole in Saigon would be slotted into place for us," said Gerber.

"That's about the size of it."

Gerber glanced at Morrow, saw the little sack again and felt a tiny bit better. "I guess the only course of action now is to head back downtown."

"Of course."

KINSON, along with the others, sat in the same small, hot conference room and waited for someone to arrive to complete their briefings. Kinson had a dozen questions he wanted answered before he agreed to the mission into Cambodia. He also wondered if anyone would balk at giving him written orders. The orders didn't have to spell out the mission, just to say that he was assigned to the task.

Burgess was restless. The man couldn't stay seated. He was up, to the door and then down again. He wandered around, looking at the pictures on the walls, at the slide projector and even at the podium, searching for something that might have been left behind. Trying to find something to occupy the minutes until the briefing officer arrived.

"You're making me nervous," said Hurtz.

"Yeah," Kinson added. "Why don't you sit down?"

Burgess looked at his watch. "How long is this guy going to keep us waiting?"

"Just a few minutes," Kinson said.

The door opened and a man entered. He walked to the podium and put his notebook on it, then moved to the slide projector, fit the carousel into the top and turned it on. For a moment he looked for the remote device and then said, "Shit. One of you is going to have to help me."

Tideman moved over and sat behind the machine. "I'll take care of it."

The man moved back to the front of the room and said, "Gentlemen, my name is Philip Reed, and I'll be conducting this briefing on the latest intelligence and the various codes you'll need for the mission. I assume that everyone here is cleared for secret material."

Kinson shrugged. "They're all going on the mission, so I guess they're cleared."

"You'll vouch for them?"

"Yes, sir."

"All right, then," said Reed. "If you'll key up the first slide."

Kinson waved a hand. "Just a moment. I'd like to know if we're going to be supplied with written orders for this."

Reed grinned, but not with friendliness or humor. "Sergeant, we do not cut orders for you to operate inside a foreign nation."

"I'm aware of that. I'd just like a document saying that I'm working out of MACV on a special assignment, in case this thing blows up in my face. Something to show that I'm not operating on my own."

Reed took a deep breath and exhaled slowly. He stared at Kinson for a moment and then looked down at the podium. "I'll make a note. You'll have the document tomorrow when you leave."

"No," said Kinson. "I don't want to take it into the field."

"I'll speak with Jerry Maxwell," snapped Reed. "He'll show you the document. Satisfied?"

Kinson didn't answer right away. Finally he grunted, "I guess I'll have to be."

Reed began again. "Now, if someone will turn on the machine."

Tideman complied, punching up the slide. He focused it and then sat back.

Then, before starting, Reed looked at his watch. He stood at the front reading over his notes, waiting. Finally the door opened again and three men entered. One of them was an American officer wearing jungle fatigues with a Special Forces patch on the shoulder. He pointed to the empty chairs and said, "You sit down."

The other two were small, dark men. They both had black hair, almond-shaped brown eyes. They wore modified fatigues, tailored to fit their slight bodies. They looked enough alike, were dressed enough alike, they could have been twins.

The American said, "Both men speak fairly good English. Speak slowly and clearly and they'll be able to follow." He then left.

As the door closed, Kinson asked, "What in the hell is this?"

"You were briefed on your Cambodian scouts."

Kinson stared at the two men and then looked at the civilian. He shrugged. "I don't know these men."

"No, but we do. They're trustworthy."

Burgess spoke up then. "Excuse me, but did I miss something? Are you going with us, Mr. Reed?"

"I'm here as the briefing officer and nothing more."

"Then your opinion of the trustworthiness of anyone doesn't mean shit. We're the ones with our butts on the line."

"I've been assured—"

"You miss the point," snapped Burgess. "If you're not going with us, a mistake here won't hurt you, but it can fucking well kill us."

"We good," said one of the men. "We kill many VC. We kill many Cong."

Burgess looked at the man and shook his head. He held up a hand as if about to wave. "Don't get me wrong, but we don't know you guys. Suddenly our lives are in your hands."

"And ours, yours," said the other Cambodian. "Our lives in your hands."

Kinson looked at the men and then to Burgess. "He's got you there."

"But . . ." Burgess realized that there was nothing more to say.

Reed interrupted. "Everyone's life depends on everyone else. I don't think we've got a problem here."

Burgess looked at the Cambodians again and then at Reed. He shrugged.

"If everyone is ready, then."

Kinson said, "Please proceed."

"Gentlemen, the information you'll be receiving here is classified as secret. Please do not discuss it outside the confines of these walls or in places where your discussion could be overheard."

"Of course," said Kinson, annoyed that the civilian felt he had to remind him of COMSEC.

Using the latest intelligence, Reed launched into an in-depth briefing on the town of Kampong Trach, just over the Cambodian border. He provided information on the population, the rivers, jungles and animal life around it. He briefed them on the proximity of the Ho Chi Minh Trail and on what the most recent aerial reconnaissance photos had shown. He detailed suspected military camps and VC strongholds in the vicinity and then talked about the best routes into and out of the area. He talked for fifty minutes without letting up, nodding at Tideman when he wanted the slides changed.

When he finished he said, "That should tell you everything you need to know about the area around Kampong Trach."

"What time do we jump off?" asked Burgess.

"Sergeant?" said Reed.

"Everyone assemble at Hotel Three at zero eight hundred." Kinson looked up to Reed. "That satisfactory?"

"I'll make a note and see that transport is there. How many men are you going to take?"

"Those you see here and three additional who weren't available for the briefing."

Reed closed his folder. "Will you need maps?"

Kinson shook his head. "We've maps. There's nothing that we'll want to have marked on them. We know the destination and we know where we'll start from. That's all we need."

Reed flipped over a page in his briefing book. "All right, I'm going to give you the radio codes, check-in times and E and E code letters. Prepare to copy this."

"We're not supposed to take that sort of information out with us."

"Then don't write it down," snapped Reed. "I don't care what you do. This is the information that could save your life."

"We'll get it all," said Kinson.

Reed stared at the sergeant and then began giving them the radio frequencies to use, the code words that had to precede each transmission and the check-in times. That finished, he went over the authentication procedures for the search-and-rescue forces. When he finished, he asked Kinson to give it all back to him. Kinson repeated it quickly and perfectly.

"All right then, if there's nothing more, you men are released until pickup tomorrow."

"What about them?" asked Burgess, pointing at the Cambodians.

Kinson snapped, "They're our allies."

"Sure, Sarge."

"They'll be escorted to Hotel Three, tomorrow. Tonight they'll stick with the Special Forces."

"Of course," said Burgess.

"You know, Sam, if you shut your fucking mouth, we could get out of here and you could make your date. And by keeping your mouth shut, you might not offend our allies, who then won't feel obligated to stick a knife in your back. That's if they have the chance. I just might beat them to it." Kinson glanced at the Cambodians and said to them, "I hope he has not offended you."

"No," said one of them. "We understand."

Reed cleared his throat. "Gentlemen?"

Kinson stood up and said, "Thank you, Mr. Reed. We'll be prepared tomorrow."

The Americans left the conference room together. In the hallway, out of earshot of Reed and the Cambodians, Kinson said, "Sam, you're a fucking jerk-off. We don't question our allies' loyalty in front of them. But we do watch them once we're in the field. That's why I opted to bring three more men. We'll be able to watch them twenty-four hours a day and we won't wear ourselves out doing it."

Burgess began to laugh. "I thought you'd forgotten where you were and what was going on around you. I thought you'd forgotten that we can't trust these people."

"I never forget anything. It's the reason I'm going home in one piece."

"Me too."

"Not if you don't wise up," Kinson said. "Not if you don't wise up."

3

THE CARASEL HOTEL
SAIGON

All the way back from the World's Largest PX, Morrow had refused to let Gerber look in the little sack. Every time he asked about it, she deflected the question by suggesting there would be something interesting on TV that night. Gerber finally gave up.

They rode in silence until the taxi driver grunted once and dived through traffic amid squealing tires and blaring horns. He jammed on the brakes in front of the Carasel Hotel, turned in the seat and grinned.

"You here."

"Yes," said Gerber. "Barely."

"You pay. Fifteen hundred P. You get good ride. Numbah-one ride."

Gerber glanced to the right at Fetterman, who sat back shaking his head slowly. "Fifteen hundred P. No way, Jack."

"You pay now."

Gerber opened the door and stepped out. He held out a hand, and Morrow grabbed it as she slid across the back seat. As she exited she looked back at Fetterman, but the master sergeant refused to budge.

"I'll give you four hundred P."

"Three pax. Fifteen hundred. Cheap."

"My man," said Fetterman. "Fifteen hundred is outrageous. It is ridiculous. It is unfair. Five hundred P, plus a healthy tip is more than adequate."

"Hey, you Cheap Charlie. You numbah ten. America numbah ten."

Fetterman grinned at the man. "You reduce the size of your tip by suggesting that my homeland is less than perfect. You hurt your own cause."

Morrow leaned close and asked, "Why is Fetterman arguing with the man?"

"Don't ever ask him that. You'll get his lecture on the inflationary spiral and how the United States, refusing to understand the local economy, moves in to wreck it. Girls, hootch maids, workers on the military bases, those cashiers we saw earlier, now earn in a single month more than their fathers earn in a year."

"What's that got to do with the price of a cab ride?" asked Morrow.

"It's all interrelated. By undercutting the local economy, by paying what we think is a fair wage as opposed to the wage dictated by the local economy, we break down the societal barriers, destroy the nuclear family and ruin the natural mores of the culture."

"All this because the cab driver wants fifteen bucks for a cab ride?"

"As I say," said Gerber, "don't ask him about it. You'll get an hour's lecture."

"Maybe there's a story in there," she said.

"If you happen to be a financial reporter or an anthropologist," said Gerber. He looked back into the cab.

"Eight hundred P and a fifty P tip," said Fetterman, tiring of the game.

The driver grinned broadly showing broken yellowed teeth. "Nine hundred P."

Fetterman took out the money and handed it to the man. He slipped across the back seat and got out. As he stood up, the cab rocketed into traffic.

"Sounds like he got the best of you, Tony," said Gerber.

"It was Tet, Captain. Man claimed his taxi was damaged in the fighting by American soldiers and we, the Americans who damaged his cab, should help pay for the repairs."

"And you bought that?"

"Oh, hell no, but I liked the originality of it. Showed the man had put some thought into it. Besides, three bucks a piece wasn't bad for us."

Gerber shifted the box holding the television from the right to the left. He held the edge of the carton with his hip, his left arm draped over it. "The plan now?"

"We go inside where it's cool," said Fetterman, "and figure it out."

"We don't even have to do that," Morrow replied. "We just go inside, change our clothes and then go to dinner."

"Good," said Gerber. "I like that."

Fetterman moved toward the double glass doors. As he did, the doorman moved to open it and he felt a blast of cold air from inside.

As he walked in he said, "I might pass on the dinner."

"Why, Tony?" asked Morrow.

"Feel like a fifth wheel. Not all that important."

"Don't you know some young lady who'd like to join us?" asked Morrow.

Fetterman hesitated. "None that we could round up quickly."

Gerber said, "Since when have you worried about being a fifth wheel. Hell, Tony, you've got to eat, and we've got to eat, and there is no sense in not eating together."

Now Fetterman smiled. "You've convinced me. Just wanted to be sure that you two didn't mind."

Morrow looked at him and then at Gerber and asked, "What in the hell is with you two? First Mack is acting mad at the world, then you start playing stupid games."

"It's the heat," said Fetterman. "The heat, pure and simple."

They walked across the marble lobby of the hotel. Huge marble pillars held up the ornate, white-and-gold ceiling. There were Victorian couches and wing-back chairs clustered in conversation pits around the floor. To one side, set back from the doors and across the lobby, was the registration desk, a teak-and-mahogany affair with two clerks working behind it. In the rear, almost out of sight of the desk, was the elevator. Little more than a gilded cage, it offered a good view of the lobby as it climbed upward.

They reached it and Fetterman said, "I'll meet the two of you down here in an hour and a half."

"Why so long?" asked Gerber.

Fetterman pointed at the television. "Give you a chance to play with your new toy and to get cleaned up. Don't want you to have to rush."

They entered the elevator and rode upward. Fetterman got off first, leaving Gerber and Morrow alone. The captain glanced at the little sack and asked again, "You going to give me a hint?"

"Nope. You'll just have to be patient. Play with your TV like Tony said."

"Thanks."

Gerber stopped the elevator and opened the door. Morrow exited and waited, then followed Gerber down the hallway. Pausing at his door, he shifted the TV around and pulled out a key. He unlocked the door and pushed it open.

Morrow entered first and walked to the air conditioner built into the wall under the window. Gerber followed. He pushed the door shut and set the TV on the floor out of the way.

"Hot in here," said Morrow.

"A little."

She sat down on the bed and looked at him. She crossed her legs slowly but didn't say a word.

"You want to use the bathroom first?" asked Gerber.

"I probably should go to my room. Change my clothes and take a bath there."

Gerber rubbed a hand over his head. He moved toward the window and said, "I'll come by your room then, in about an hour?"

"Sure." But she didn't move.

"Something wrong?"

Morrow stood up. "No. I guess not." She stepped to the door. "About an hour."

Gerber followed her to the door and stopped her before she could open it. He turned her and kissed once, on the lips. He felt her respond, pressing herself against him. He could feel the dampness on the back of her dress.

He pulled away and asked, "You sure you don't want to tell me what's in the bag?"

She laughed. "Not now." Without waiting, she opened the door and stepped into the hall. She turned and waved, and then hurried away.

REED WATCHED as the soldiers filed out of the briefing room, leaving the two Cambodians with him. He didn't know what to do about them and stood staring at them. A few moments later, the door opened and the Special Forces officer who had brought them in returned.

"The plan from here?" he asked.

"They have to be at Hotel Three by eight tomorrow."

"No problem."

"Where're they going to be tonight?"

One of the Cambodes looked at Reed and said, "We talk your language."

"Of course," said Reed.

The officer said, "We'll head back to our compound at Long Binh and then fly into Hotel Three tomorrow."

"You'll be with them all night?"

The SF man looked at Reed, stared at him and then said, "More or less."

"Fine." Reed gathered his papers and got out of the room. He headed down the hall, descended a flight of stairs and stopped at the iron gate that blocked off part of the basement. The armed MP, a bored young man, looked up, recognized Reed and unlocked the gate. He returned to his magazine without saying a word.

Maxwell wasn't in the office when Reed arrived. He opened the safe, stuffed his report into the working papers file and then opened the bottom drawer. He set the slide tray in there and kicked the drawer shut. Finished, he made sure that all the drawers were closed and the safe was locked.

He sat down for a moment and then realized if he stayed long enough for Maxwell to return, Maxwell might find something else for him to do. He grabbed a sheet of paper and wrote a quick note, telling Maxwell that Kinson wanted something in writing. Anything, so long as it would cover his butt in case things didn't go well. He tried to keep it generic so that someone finding it and reading it wouldn't understand, but not so convoluted that Maxwell couldn't.

Then, feeling that his job was done, he stood and moved to the door, hesitating there as if he was afraid that Maxwell was lurking just outside. He opened it, found the hall empty, and then hurried back to the gate.

The MP looked up again and asked, "Leaving for the night?"

"I guess so."

When the MP pushed a clipboard at him, Reed took it, signed his name and then the time. Finished, he waited for the MP to open the gate, afraid that Maxwell would appear at any moment, but managed to get up the stairs and to the double doors leading to the exit without the CIA man finding him.

Stepping out of the building into the heat of the late afternoon, he stood there looking out on the expanse of green lawn where a group of soldiers, walking shoulder to shoulder, moved along picking up the trash. Beyond them was the MP post, a sandbagged, bunkerlike affair with an armed guard. He was covered by another concealed post.

Reed walked down the sidewalk, past the flagpole and into the graveled parking lot. He climbed into the driver's seat of a jeep and then leaped back out. Anyone who had been in Vietnam for more than a day should have learned that the tropical sun heated everything super hot. He stood there looking at the seat. It seemed inviting, but he knew that was a trick. It was an evil thing, waiting to burn the skin from his body.

Finally Reed slipped behind the wheel, holding his butt off the seat with his legs and his shoulders, which were pressed into the backrest. He lowered himself slowly, like a man getting into a bath that was too hot for him. He took it by stages, forgetting that Maxwell could appear at any moment to call him back to work.

He fished the key out of the pocket of his civilian pants, used it to unlock the chain and drop it to the floor. He switched on the engine, sat there in a stiff position, waiting for the heat to evaporate from the seat. He'd learned the trick when he lived in California. When he could lean back without burning himself, he backed from the stall and entered traffic.

At first he was going downtown, but decided he was too easy to find down there. Maxwell had a habit of showing up at his door and telling him that he was needed back at MACV for

some vital last-minute work. Or Maxwell sent someone to call
for him and bring him back.

He turned down a wide boulevard filled with traffic and pedestrians. Thousands of people milling around with nothing
better to do than line the sidewalks and hold out their grimy
hands to ask for money. Some were veterans missing an arm
or leg. Some were children, trying to get enough to eat. Others were women trying to support children now that their
husbands were gone, killed in the war or missing in action.
And there were those who were just hustlers, believing that
begging was a legitimate alternative to working.

Reed had no time for any of them. They were wasting their
lives. Passing the time, day to day, hoping for food and a place
to sleep, and not worrying about a contribution to society.
Selfish people who could see no farther than the end of their
own noses.

The blare of a horn frightened him from his thoughts. He
saw a cab veer close again, trying to force its way into the tiny
space between him and the truck in front. Reed eased down
the accelerator and flipped the Vietnamese driver the bird.

He pulled to the side then and turned down a narrower
street. This one was lined with poles that held dozens of wires.
The pavement became rough, potholed and broken. There
were ditches on both sides filled with stagnant water. The
houses, many built during the French rule, were old and di-
lapidated. Some had broken windows repaired with plywood.
Paint was peeling, and the tile of the roofs was broken. Walls
that had been damaged during the Tet fighting had never been
repaired.

Children played in the dirt in front of the houses, or in the
water in the ditches. Dirty ragged children, some of them
completely naked, ran around chasing each other.

Reed pulled to the end of the street where one of the nicer
houses stood. There were pockmarks on the walls from bullets, and one window had yet to be repaired, but it was a neater

house. There were plantings around it, a palm at one side and a couple of bushes with giant bright green leaves on either side of the front door.

Sitting in front of the house was another jeep. It belonged to another of the civilians working at MACV. Reed grinned as he thought about it. Gary Pittman had introduced Reed to the woman who lived in the house. She had smiled at him, and he knew in that moment she was no longer interested in Pittman. She stayed with him for the money, for the protection he offered, but she didn't like him.

Reed drove on by, and then stopped down the block. He backed up so that his jeep was concealed in a thick planting of bright green bushes with huge plastic-looking leaves. He could watch the house.

A few minutes later Pittman left the house. He stopped once, turned and waved, and then continued to his jeep. He climbed behind the wheel, waved at the house again and then drove off. He didn't look right or left as he did, driving past Reed without noticing him.

"Idiot," Reed said as he started his own jeep. He didn't understand how anyone could be so stupid. She was using him, pure and simple. Sometimes they laughed about the things he told her. Laughed at his plans and his feelings and his sexual habits. He liked it straight and that was all. Man on top getting it done quickly.

Pittman had no class. Reed stopped in front of her house, locked the jeep by using the chain and looping it through the steering wheel. As he jumped out, he put a hand up to shade his eyes, figuring that the sun would be gone before he got back to the jeep. The seat shouldn't be hot enough to fry chicken when he returned.

He walked up to the door, but before he could knock, it opened again. Peeking around the edge was a single, almond-shaped eye. He could see long black hair and little else.

"Hello, Philip."

The voice was light, feminine, and Reed felt his intestines grow cold.

"Hi."

She opened the door and stepped back, allowing him to enter the house. He turned and looked at her. A young Vietnamese woman, no more than twenty, no more than five feet tall with jet black hair that hung to her waist. She was a slight girl, almost delicate, with the features of a china doll. She had big eyes of a liquid brown that Reed felt lost in. She was the most beautiful girl he had ever seen, and he thought he would do anything for her. At least anything if he could do it in the next five minutes.

"You come and sit," she said.

"Of course, Thi. I'll come and sit. Did you have fun with Gary?"

"He is a pig. I don't like him."

"Then why put up with him?"

Now she smiled. "Because he buys this." She held up her hands to indicate the house. "Because he promises many things. And because he brought you."

"Someday we'll have to get rid of him. I don't like hiding outside until he finishes."

She ignored that. "You would like some tea?"

"I'd like a shot of bourbon. A big, tall bourbon so dark that it'd look like I was drinking tea."

"I go get." She spun and left him standing in the doorway to the living room where he could finally sit down as she had invited him to do. He watched her disappear, knowing that he hadn't surprised her. She was dressed in a miniskirt and a light, white blouse. She had been waiting for him. Waiting for him while Pittman sat in her house, but she had managed to get Pittman out before too long.

He dropped into a stiff uncomfortable chair upholstered in light blue. It didn't match the rest of the decor. Across from him was a couch, and over it a long dirty mirror. His image in it was a ghostly form, only vaguely human.

Near a rear window was a PX record player and a stack of albums, many of which he had contributed. On the walls around him were various pictures of the family and of Jesus Christ, most showing a glow around his head like a halo. Thi's family was Catholic.

She returned with a tray holding two glasses, both beaded with moisture. She knelt in front of him, holding up the tray, allowing him to select one of the glasses. When he had done that, she took the other and set the tray aside on the hard-wood floor.

Reed reached down and touched the top of her head, stroking her much the way he would a good dog.

"A hard day?" she asked.

He looked down at her. "Your command of the English language never ceases to amaze me."

"If the French were still here, I would speak French. Now it's the Americans, so I speak English. But you have not answered my question."

"Not rough, just tiring. Briefings that had to be prepared quickly. I spent the morning researching some Cambodian town called Kampong Trach. Had to learn everything about it."

"I don't believe I know of the place."

Reed drank deeply and sighed. "No reason you should. Little place, north and west of Tay Ninh. No easy way to get there short of walking."

She leaned forward, her cheek against his knee. "I don't want to hear any more about this place."

Again Reed drank, feeling the liquor spreading through his belly, calming him. "And I had to work with these two Cambodians today. Dirty, disgusting men who couldn't speak much English. Hard little men."

She looked up at him. "You judge people by their command of English?"

"No, of course not. It was just one more irritant. Talking to them about this little town and not knowing if they were understanding a word I was saying. Trying to explain how to avoid the swamps so that they could...well, never mind that."

She stood up then and pulled at his hand. "You are tired and dirty. Just like your little Cambodian friends. We shall bath you. Clean you."

Reed let himself be pulled to his feet and followed her upstairs. He finished his drink in the bathroom and set the glass down out of the way.

"You may begin," he said.

And then, surprising him, she stripped first.

THEY ATE DINNER in the fanciest of the three restaurants in the hotel. Gerber, holding true to form, ordered a steak and baked potato. Fetterman and Morrow were more adventurous, ordering from the seafood platter, getting a variety of fish and crustaceans. They traded bits while Gerber worked on demolishing his steak all by himself. They had wine and they had dessert, and after nearly two hours they could eat no more. Fetterman called for the bill and insisted on paying the whole thing himself. When Gerber balked, the sergeant pressed the point.

"My treat, sir. You've bought me dinner more than once. I thought it was time to repay you."

"Well, I make it a policy never to turn down free food. Thank you."

"Yes," said Morrow, leaning over and kissing Fetterman on the cheek. "Thank you."

Fetterman grinned. "Now you know why I said I'd pay."

They left the restaurant, and Fetterman headed to his room. Just before the sergeant disappeared, Gerber called, "I don't want to learn that you've been over at MACV volunteering us for anything dangerous.''

"Would I do that?" asked Fetterman innocently.

"More often than not."

Fetterman waved at him. "I'll try to be good this time."

As Fetterman disappeared around a corner, Gerber and Morrow entered the elevator and took it up to her room. She had left the air conditioner running so that it was comfortable inside. She turned on the lights, moved to the window to close the curtains and then turned, facing him.

"Is it time?" he asked.

She bit her bottom lip and then nodded. "Yes. I think it's time."

"Do I get to see into the sack first?"

"I think not. I'll just don the garb and model it."

Gerber sat down on the bed. "That sounds fine."

She pointed to the side where there was a small kitchen area. There was a table covered with papers and files and surrounded by four chairs. In front of one of the chairs was a manual typewriter.

"I've some Beam's in there."

"I've had enough alcohol for a while."

She stopped at the bathroom door with a mock frown on her face. "Did I hear you right?"

"We're not required to drink ourselves under the table every night," said Gerber.

"Well, excuse me." Then she smiled and said, "I'll be back in a minute."

Gerber turned and pulled a pillow out from under the sheet and propped it against the wall. The small room was like his, with the exception of the kitchen area. The decor, the window with a blackout curtain, the wooden wardrobe against the wall, the slowly turning ceiling fan, and the double bed matched what was in his.

He laced his fingers under his head and stared up at the ceiling, wondering what Morrow could have crammed into the tiny sack. It didn't look as if there had been much in it. Of course she could supplement it with something she already owned if she wanted to. She already owned a couple of things that were designed to set the mind on fire.

And then the question was answered. The bathroom door swung open to reveal her standing there practically naked. There was so little cloth in the costume that he wondered why she had bothered with anything at all. And the little that he could see did nothing to hide her body.

But when she walked into the room, he understood why she had bothered. The wisps of cloth accented her body perfectly. Naturally there was a garter belt and stockings. She wore black lace bikini panties that were almost nonexistent and that he could see right through. There was a bra of some type that barely concealed her nipples but that did nothing to hide the shape of her breasts. Nothing to hide her body and everything to accent it.

"Well," she asked. "What do you think?" She turned slowly, giving him the full view.

The panties seemed to disappear in the back. There was a tiny belt for the garter and a string for the bra and nothing else. From the rear she looked to be almost totally naked. It was an amazing thing to see.

She faced him again and Gerber felt himself respond. He hadn't known that clothes, or rather, the lack of them could be so stimulating. He shifted around, hoping that she wouldn't see his response. He wished she would turn again, giving him a chance to adjust himself.

"Well?"

Gerber let his eyes climb her slowly, starting with the trim ankles encased in the nearly invisible stockings, up to her naked thighs where the stockings ended. His eyes lingered at her hips as he tried to see if the panties failed to cover anything.

He studied her from the hips to the shoulders and finally stopped on her face.

"That is probably the most provocative costume I've almost seen."

"You like it?"

"Robin, it is a lethal weapon. You could kill wearing it. I don't think it's fair. You show up anywhere dressed like that, and you'd own the world."

"But do you like it?"

"Yes, Robin, I like it. I love it. If I had a camera, I'd photograph it. I'd take slides and charge admission for those who'd like to see it."

She walked toward him, stopped at the edge of the bed and asked, "Really?"

"Really. Now come here before I explode."

She grinned and did as he asked.

4

HOTEL THREE
TAN SON NHUT

Kinson stood in the doorway of the terminal, looking out on the grass and concrete pads that made up the heliport called Hotel Three. His rucksack lay on the cement near the door. He held his rifle in his right hand and had a bandolier of extra ammo in his left.

He still wasn't happy about going on the mission, but he had been assured that written orders, attaching him to MACV for the duration of the mission, had been issued. A courier had brought them, and Kinson had locked them in his footlocker. If something went wrong, then he would be covered. Partially.

"Soon?" asked Burgess.

"Very soon," said Kinson. "I'm not sure how we're supposed to know which chopper, though."

"Someone will let us know. You should sit down and relax."

Kinson rubbed his forehead and then looked at the sweat on his hand. "Eight in the morning and I'm already sweating like a pig. It's going to be a hot mother."

Burgess moved closer, glanced over his shoulder at the Cambodians and at Tideman. "I don't trust those guys."

"You said that yesterday."

"Well, now I've had the chance to think about it, I still don't trust them. You find out where they spent the night?"

Now Kinson looked at his men. Tideman and Hurtz were sticking near the Cambodes, as were three other men that Kinson had recruited. Hernandez, Wilson and Barnes, all privates with four to six months in-country. Competent soldiers who saw their roles in the Vietnam conflict as surviving to return home. They sat on a broken-down, threadbare green couch, their equipment on the dirty floor in front of their feet.

Finally Kinson replied, "With the Special Forces at Long Binh. There was no time for them to contact friends in the VC, if they have friends in the VC to contact. Besides, they're Cambodes and they hate the Vietnamese."

"They could have told their friends on the camp who'll pass the word later."

Kinson shrugged. "Nothing we can do about it now. We'll just have to keep our eyes and ears open."

"Christ, you're calm about this. They saddle us with two guys we don't know and send us on a cross-border—"

"Will you shut the fuck up?" Kinson looked around quickly and saw that no one was listening to them. "Why don't you take an ad out in the paper? Tell the whole fucking world what we're doing."

"You know what I mean."

Before Kinson could reply, another chopper landed, the sound of the engines wiping away the conversation. Kinson ducked his head and closed his eyes in anticipation of the rotor wash, but the windstorm didn't develop. The helicopter landed fifty yards away and then hovered to one of the pads, dropping to the ground there.

The Spec Five, sitting behind the waist-high counter in front of the scheduling board, yelled, "Kinson, that's your ride."

"Thanks." He turned and shouted, "Let's go, men." He picked up his rucksack, shouldered it and then waited for his men. The group headed out, heads down, ducking under the spinning blades of the Huey.

Kinson put a foot on the skid and then climbed into the cargo compartment of the chopper. As the rest of the men scrambled in, sitting on the red troop seat or on the floor, Kinson crouched between the pilots' seats. He unfolded his map and spread it on the console there.

"You guys know where we're going?" shouted Kinson.

The copilot looked at him, pointed at his ear and shook his head. Kinson leaned closer and shouted the question again.

"Doesn't matter. We're landing at Tay Ninh to refuel. You can tell us what you need then."

Kinson shrugged and nodded. He folded his map and put it away. As he turned and sat down on the deck, the chopper came up off its skids. A moment later they were climbing over the chain-link fence that separated Hotel Three from the rest of Tan Son Nhut.

Through the cargo compartment doors, Kinson watched as Tan Son Nhut dropped away. Jet aircraft sat on the parallel runways. There were revetments to protect the fighters on the ground, and metal hangars lined the runways and taxiways. It was a bright scene, almost everything built of corrugated metal or painted white. The sunlight seemed to reflect off everything, gaining in intensity as it blazed upward.

Kinson turned his attention to the countryside. He had heard that given the number of flights in and out, if Hotel Three was lumped in, Tan Son Nhut was the world's busiest airport. Just outside the fences that protected it were rice paddies where farmers used water buffalo to plow. People lived in thatched hootches without the benefit of indoor plumbing and electricity. The whole family lived in one room, ate rice boiled from a huge black pot over a fire and watched as modern technology laid waste to everything around them.

He settled against the back of the pilot's seat where he didn't have to look outside. As they reached altitude for their trip to Tay Ninh, Kinson relaxed. The air blowing in the open doors was cool. The sweat dried quickly, and in a few moments it was almost cold in the chopper. Kinson looked at his men and then tilted his head back against the hard ceramic of the armored seat and closed his eyes. There was nothing to worry about until they reached Tay Ninh, a good thirty minutes away.

And then, there wasn't anything to worry about there, either. Just pick an LZ that looked promising, move five or six klicks away from it and wait for nightfall. It'd be twenty-four hours before there was anything to worry about.

That's what he told himself, but somehow he just couldn't bring himself to believe it.

REED ROLLED OVER and glanced up at the bright window. Sunlight was streaming in, heating the tiny bedroom. He was alone in bed, Thi having sneaked away earlier. He reached to the right, where a small black lacquered table stood, and picked up his watch. He blinked, trying to focus on the tiny numbers, but his sleep-blurred eyes were making it impossible.

Thi entered then, carrying a small tray that held two steaming cups. She crouched next to him and smiled. "It is a good morning."

Reed groaned and rolled onto his back. "You should have awakened me. I'm going to be late now."

She stood up and dropped the silk robe she had been wearing. Now she was completely naked. A slight body with small breasts and not an ounce of fat on her. She stood, hands on her hips, looking down at him.

"Maybe I don't care if I'm late," he said, changing his mind. "What are they going to do, send me to Vietnam?" He had heard soldiers say that dozens of times, indicating that there was nothing worse that could happen. It could only get better.

"You want coffee?" she asked.

"Yes," he said, nodding for emphasis. "I need coffee." He sat up and let the sheet drop away so that he was naked to the waist. He propped up a pillow and took the cup from her, wondering where in the hell she had gotten her energy. Before he had arrived in Vietnam, he'd been warned about the women, but it had been his impression that the warning had only encompassed prostitutes and not the common everyday women. He had thought they had been brought up to be proper, with a distaste for sex, but maybe someone had forgotten to tell Thi. She was a wildcat who tried to suck every ounce of fluid from his body.

As he drank, he thought about the night before. They had barely gotten up the stairs and she was out of her clothes. She shed them as they walked down the hall to the bathroom and then had crouched naked to turn on the water. It was in that moment, staring at her naked flesh, that he had known he was lost. He would have done anything at that point.

But there had been nothing to do, except take off his own clothes. Before they got into the water, she had stood and turned to face him. Raising up on tiptoes, she had tilted her head to be kissed. Reed had stepped close to do just that, but she had reached down to take him in her hand. She gently tugged, moved, and he felt himself slip inside. She had begun to rock her hips back and forth, and Reed had thought he had died and gone to heaven.

Finally she had coaxed him down on the floor, Reed on his back. She straddled him and sat down. She then began to move, controlling the situation. She leaned back, her hands on his knees, her long hair dragging on the floor. Her movements became more rapid as she lost herself in what she was doing, her breath coming in short bursts as her excitement built.

She screamed once, whipped her head forward and then doubled over. She hugged him and then started to move again, bringing him along slowly.

Reed let her do it then. He lay on his back, his hands on her, cupping her and helping her as she worked on him. Slowly at first, and then faster as he began to move his hips in time to her. He closed his eyes and let her take him to the top until he exploded. Then he collapsed, the breath rasping in his throat as she moved her legs, straightening them so that she could stretch out on his body.

That hadn't been the end of it. They had bathed and talked about dinner, but instead had gone into the bedroom. He'd taken control that time, she under him as he braced himself on his elbows to keep his weight off her. They worked at it, slowly at first and then faster and faster until both were breathing hard and were covered with a light coating of sweat.

It was long after midnight when they finally gave up, both of them exhausted. Reed's body hurt, and he was sure that he was close to dying. He had been rubbed raw. But he didn't care. Completely drained, he had fallen asleep and had not moved until he had awakened alone.

He sipped the coffee she had brought, looking at her over the rim of the cup. She sat naked on the bed, the sunlight playing across her body, highlighting her breasts. Her nipples were erect and her lips were soft and pouting.

"No," said Reed. "Please. No more."

"Ever?"

"I need a moment, a day to recover." He took a long drink, draining the cup.

"You are weak." She grinned broadly, coyly.

"No, not weak. Sore."

"So what we do now?"

Shaking his head, Reed said, "I never thought I would say it, but you put on your robe and I'll get dressed. I've got to get to work sometime this morning."

"But you come back."

"Oh yeah, baby, I'll come back. I'll definitely come back."

She got up, bent down to get the robe, but kept her legs straight, giving him an almost obscene view of her. Then, still grinning, she turned and slowly put on her robe.

When she had finished, he asked, "Is it too late to change my mind?"

"No."

He laughed. "My brain says yes but my body says no. Tonight. After we eat maybe, but definitely not now."

"You are the boss," she said.

"That's what you think." He threw off the sheet and stood up facing her. "A shower."

"Alone?"

"We'd better make it alone. If I'm to live through the day."

"Then please go ahead."

Reed left the room and headed for the bathroom. As he entered the shower, he didn't know that she was going through the pockets of his pants, searching for his wallet. If he had known, he would have been disappointed but not terribly upset. There wasn't anything for her to find except some money, and he didn't care about it. If it took money to get into her pants, then he was willing to pay the price. She was more than worth it.

THEY LANDED AT TAY NINH in the POL point, but they didn't shut down. The crew chief and door gunner had gotten out to refuel the aircraft, while the pilots sat up front watching the other aircraft around them.

Kinson got out his map again, laid it on the console and shouted over the noise from the turbine, "I've got an LZ picked out."

The aircraft commander picked up the map and examined it. Kinson leaned over and pointed, "We need to touch down somewhere in this area."

The man turned and shouted back. "That's a fairly rough area. Scattered LZs and trees that are two hundred feet tall."

"Can you get in there?"

"Yeah, but I'm not sure that I want to. It's not like the terrain to the south, which is wide open."

Kinson nodded but didn't understand the pilot's reluctance. If there were LZs, why didn't they want to hit them?

"We'll have to wait a few minutes for the guns to arrive," shouted the man, breaking into his thoughts.

"Why gunships? We're supposed to sneak in there, not announce our arrival."

The pilot shifted around so that he could face Kinson. "And I'm not going into that area without gun support. Charlie operates in there with ease, has almost every LZ ringed with bunkers, and sometimes just sits in them waiting for helicopters to land."

That took Kinson by surprise. He leaned over, his face closer to the pilot's. "I wasn't told about that in my briefings."

"They're not manned all the time. But Charlie knows what we need for an LZ."

"Maybe there's a place you can get a single ship into."

"Shit, with those trees, the first third to one half of the LZ is unusable. We have to be careful we don't get into settling with power and crash."

That was also something new. Kinson had never heard of settling with power. He'd never heard about unusable portions of LZs. Suddenly the mission had taken on added danger, and they hadn't even gotten into the field.

"What do you recommend?"

"Staying here," said the aircraft commander seriously.

"And if we can't do that?"

The man took the map and studied. "Where is your final destination?"

"That's classified," said Kinson, feeling like an asshole. It was the sort of answer that the heroes in war movies gave to their girlfriends, not something that took place in real life.

"Fine," said the pilot, dropping the map.

"Listen," yelled Kinson, "we need to hit the ground anywhere in this general vicinity. We can get to where we're going from there."

"You want to get close to the border?"

"Why?"

"Because the NVA have fifty-caliber and thirty-seven millimeter weapons set up all along it, waiting for aircraft to get within a klick or two." He reached back along the console to the map case and pulled out one of the aeronautical charts. He pointed to a legend along the Cambodian border. Kinson read it.

"Overflight requires diplomatic clearance," it said in bold red letters.

"Three, four klicks away will be fine."

"Then we'll put you down about here."

Kinson looked at it and nodded. "Fine." He picked up his map and turned around, sitting on the deck of the chopper. The door gunner finished the refueling, slid the side door back and used a cotter pin to lock it in place in the open position. Then both he and the crew chief got back in, taking their places behind the M-60s.

They picked up to a hover, moved off to the side and set down again. A moment later two gunships hovered by, moving into a position for takeoff, and Kinson's aircraft came back up to a hover. They lifted off over the perimeter and the wire, flying over the bunkers that protected Tay Ninh from the enemy, up over the palm trees that made the setting look almost romantic, the huge palms and flowing bushes that hid the thatch-and-mud hootches in a tropical setting.

They climbed out to the south and then turned, heading back to the north. Out the door was Nui Ba Den, the Black

Virgin Mountain. It rose from the flat landscape to dominate the surrounding area. East of it were jungles and forests, and to the south and west were rice paddies and farms.

They left the area of rice paddies and flew over a jungle so thick there were only a few breaks in the canopy. Off to the right, three straight lines of bomb craters showed where B-52s had dropped their loads. The ground had been ripped up and turned over. The bottoms of the craters contained water that reflected the sunlight—three long red scars in an otherwise bright green landscape.

The crew chief leaned out of his well and yelled, "We're about three minutes out."

Kinson held up a thumb. He didn't have to say a word to his men. They began to struggle into their gear, buckling the pistol belts and adjusting the straps of their rucksacks. Kinson chambered a round and flipped on the safety.

"One minute," yelled the crew chief.

Kinson slipped closer to the open door. He looked down and watched the trees flash by, a blur of dark green that had no shape or definition.

When they were just over the tops of the trees, it seemed that they had picked up speed. Ahead there was a small opening, a clearing that didn't look to be large enough for a helicopter. But they continued toward it.

"Thirty seconds."

Now they were closer to the break in the trees. The gunships were on each side of the chopper, slightly behind it. Kinson could see the pilots through the windshield, the gunners holding their weapons pointed rearward from the cargo compartment.

"Here we go," yelled the crew chief.

Suddenly the nose came up and then slipped over to the left. The pilot sucked in some pitch and Kinson was forced down toward the bottom of the aircraft. They seemed to fall to the left, and then the pilot leveled the skids and they dropped through the opening in the trees, settling four or five feet above a rough LZ covered with tall grass and short, skinny trees.

"Go," yelled the crew chief. "Go!"

Kinson climbed out on the skid, crouched and looked down into the grass. He could see the ground, the grass flattened outward by the hurricane force of the rotor wash. Loose grass, dirt, dried leaves and weeds were sucked up and swirled around.

Kinson dropped to the ground and fell to his knees. He scrambled forward a few feet and then lay still. Off to his left dropped Hurtz and then Burgess. The others should be dropping from the other side of the helicopter, but he couldn't see them.

He glanced back over his shoulder as the chopper began a climb straight up. The nose dropped slightly and the aircraft moved forward. It seemed to barely clear the trees and then disappeared. They were left in the absolute quiet now that the helicopters were gone.

Kinson hesitated, waiting for the enemy to suddenly open fire, but nothing happened. There didn't seem to be anyone around them.

Kinson got to his feet and waved the men forward. They ran across the LZ, toward the trees on the western end. Kinson reached them first and dropped to the ground. He turned and watched as his men joined him. They were all there, including the two Cambodians.

As the men reached the trees, Kinson said, "Burgess, take the point. Hurtz right behind him. Set up security about five yards deep and then wait."

Burgess had crouched near him, no more than a foot away. Kinson could see the sweat already beaded on the other man's face, and could smell his breath.

"Shouldn't the Cambodes take the point?"

"Not until I get a look at the map. I'll put one of them on point when we move out."

"Got it." Burgess got up and moved into the trees, dodging the waist-high bushes and smaller saplings. He vanished, although Kinson could hear him moving for a couple of seconds.

Slinging his rifle, Kinson took out his map and tried to orient himself, but found it impossible. There were no terrain features, no rises or streams or swamps. Just endless jungle. Moving off to the west was their only choice. They would have to cross a stream, and there were indications that the ground was anything but flat. A klick away, he should be able to see something that would tell him exactly where he was.

He moved then, slipping to the right where one of the Cambodians knelt watching the LZ. "You take point. Head to the west."

"I know town. I go there."

"Fine," said Kinson. "You go there."

The group moved forward, the men falling in behind without having to be told. Kinson was looking for Burgess, but it seemed the big man had vanished.

And then a voice hissed, "Here."

Kinson dropped to a knee, turned to look and whispered. "Come here."

Burgess slipped out of hiding and asked, "Now what?"

"Take the point with this guy. Let him lead, but use your compass so that we make sure we're heading to the west. Keep a close watch on him."

"Got it."

"We'll fall in behind you."

Burgess nodded. He tapped the Cambodian on the shoulder and said, "Lead on, chief."

As the two of them moved off, Kinson turned and said, "Hurtz, bring up the rear with Tideman."

"Got it."

Kinson got to his feet and fell in behind Hernandez as the squad spread out. He ducked under a low branch, thought about how hot it was in the jungle and then forgot about it. There were too many other things he had to worry about. The heat and humidity weren't among them.

"Just five days," he told himself. "One hundred and twenty hours and then back to Saigon." He didn't think about the enemy or ambushes. He just concentrated on the time and the jungle around him, hoping that he could survive it. That had worked for him before, and he was sure it would work again.

5

MACV HEADQUARTERS
SAIGON

It was the middle of the afternoon before Reed could get to MACV. He drove his jeep slowly, knowing that everyone there would be aware he was late. As he pulled into the parking lot, he rejected another excuse as being something that a college student would use when he was late with a paper. It wasn't something that an adult would try.

After he locked the steering wheel, he decided that maybe the best course would be to pretend he was returning from lunch. Let everyone think he'd been working somewhere else during the morning. Not apologize for being so late. Pretend that in reality he was on time.

He hopped out of the jeep and walked up toward the double doors. Before he could reach them he was sweating heavily, and the clean clothes he'd put on only an hour earlier were soaked. Large stains under the arms and down the back turned his white shirt tan. He wiped at the sweat, wondering why he had ever been interested in Vietnam. It was his own fault that he was assigned to MACV in Vietnam.

He opened the door, moved into the first hallway and fell back against the wall, letting the breeze from the air-conditioning blow over him. He couldn't help smiling at the pain that seemed to radiate from his groin. Thi had given him quite a workout.

He pushed away from the wall and walked slowly down the corridor, descended to the lower level and then stopped at the iron gate. The MP, who recognized Reed but was not the same man who had been on duty before, said, "A little late today."

"I was over at the embassy." Reed bent over, signed his name on the clipboard and then added the date and the time. "I see Maxwell is in."

"Came in about seven and has been at it ever since." He took back the clipboard and opened the gate so that Reed could enter.

Reed hurried down the hall, stopped in front of Maxwell's door, which had no number or sign, and knocked once.

"Come."

He opened it and stepped in. Maxwell was sitting at his desk, working on a report, a Coke can near his hand. Reed realized that he had seen Coke cans stacked all over Maxwell's office but had never seen the man drink one.

Maxwell looked up. "Where in the hell have you been?"

"Here and there," said Reed. His idea of pretending that he wasn't late had already fallen apart. Maxwell wasn't going to take any shit.

"Here and there doesn't cut it, mister. I've been trying to locate you all morning. We've work to do."

Reed closed the door and slipped into the chair by Maxwell's desk. He stared at the older man and wondered why he was so upset. He hadn't been doing anything wrong, and he hadn't been doing anything that anyone else wouldn't have done, given half the chance.

"Hey, take it easy," said Reed.

Maxwell tossed down his pencil. "Don't give me shit. I've spent the morning covering your ass. Someone had to see that our patrol got off on time, and when you didn't show, I had to drive over to Tan Son Nhut. It took me thirty minutes to learn that Kinson got out on time.''

''No big thing.''

''Reed, will you shut the fuck up before you get into more trouble. While I was fucking around at Tan Son Nhut, General Cocker was looking for me to brief him on the build up in the Eye Corps area. I couldn't do that, because I was doing your job while you were out fucking around. Making sure that Kinson got his written orders so he'd feel comfortable going into Kampong Trach.''

''I guess the general gets his briefing late,'' said Reed.

''So where in the fuck were you?''

Reed thought about it for a moment. He thought of making something up. He could say that he was at the embassy doing some research and then thought, What the hell.

''I found myself a friend and we spent the night together. I just couldn't get started in the morning.''

Maxwell threw down his pencil and stared at Reed. ''You might possibly be the dumbest son of a bitch to walk through that door in the last year.''

''Hey,'' snapped Reed, ''I don't have to listen to this. I spent the night with a woman. So fucking what? I didn't call in. Well, she doesn't have a phone and it's not like I can plug into the military system at the corner. I was irresponsible and I'm sorry, but get the fuck off my back.''

''From this moment on, you will leave some kind of address or phone number for us. First, in case we have to get in touch with you, but secondly, in case something happens. It's not unheard of for the VC to kidnap officials if they get the opportunity. That will give us a starting point.''

Reed nodded. ''I'm sorry. I didn't think.''

''That's the quickest way to get killed around here,'' said Maxwell.

THEY HAD PUSHED forward all morning through the thick jungle to the west. It had been hot, tiring work. The jungle seemed to resist them, making it more difficult to travel. With the heat and humidity held in by the triple canopy, it was almost impossible to make any progress.

They had moved quickly at first, fighting the jungle, but within minutes they had slowed. There was no reason to hurry, and with the sun overhead, streaming through breaks in the canopy to turn the jungle into a glowing green hell, it was obvious they would have to conserve their strength. There were only patches of direct sun, but the rays were heating the upper layers so that it radiated downward to bake them. The humidity added to the discomfort. They were soaked as thoroughly as they would have been in the rain.

After thirty minutes, Kinson called a halt. They scattered in a loose circle for security and tried to relax, rest, but that was nearly impossible. It was too hot and humid. And Kinson was worried that the enemy had heard the helicopter land and would be out searching for them.

Kinson drank some of his water, sloshing it around in his mouth. It tasted of metal and Halozone. He swallowed it and put the canteen away. After ten minutes he decided it was time to get moving. He ordered the pointmen out, and they started off again.

They stayed in the jungle, avoiding the clearings they came to. Sometimes the undergrowth faded away so that the going was easier. The light carpet of rotting vegetation prevented the tangle of ferns, bushes, vines and weeds from taking hold. It was almost as if the canopy grew together to form a roof so that it might keep the sunlight out.

In other places it was a patchwork, with squares of sunlight pouring through. Here and there, wisps of fog drifted about, looking as if portions of the jungle had caught fire and were smoldering.

They stayed at it, moving in short bursts, stopping to rest frequently, listening for signs of pursuit. Monkeys chattered in the trees, leaping among the branches. Birds called to one another and the insects kept up a continuous buzzing, darting in toward the eyes and ears. Once Kinson spotted a flash of movement and saw a snake slithering away from them.

They stopped at noon, ate a quick cold meal and then headed out again. They moved slowly, winding toward the Cambodian border. They crossed a shallow stream and rested on the far bank. Burgess fell in, getting himself wet. If he hadn't stirred up a huge cloud of silt, Kinson wouldn't have cared. The drifting silt could tell the enemy that someone had crossed the stream if they found it.

Throughout the afternoon they slowly worked their way to the west. Kinson stopped frequently, checking his map and letting the men rest. He consulted with the Cambodes, who told him they were going in the right direction. They were getting close.

Late in the afternoon Kinson called a halt. He spread the men out in a rough circle and told them he wanted half alert. One man could rest, eat or sleep while the other watched for the enemy.

He let the afternoon fade, the sunlight slipping to the horizon and then disappearing completely. Kinson had hoped the heat would evaporate, but that didn't happen. The canopy held it in, and there was no breeze. Even with the sun gone, it was as hot and miserable as it had been during the day. It might even be considered worse since the setting sun had hinted at relief but provided none.

When it was completely dark, Kinson moved among the men and told them that it was time. He rotated the point, deciding that he didn't trust any of the others to take it now. He told one of the Cambodes to stick close to him. Burgess was given the rear and told to keep up to the rest.

They moved slowly, and Kinson wasn't sure when they crossed into Cambodia. There were no guard towers, no fences, nothing to indicate that they had moved from South Vietnam into Cambodia. But when they stopped to look at the map, Kinson crawling under a poncho liner and using a flashlight to check their position, he decided they were no longer in South Vietnam.

About midnight they stopped for twenty minutes, the men fanning out and drinking a little of their water. Finally Kinson got them up again, wanting to get into position near Kampong Trach by sunrise. Then they could decide what they needed to do.

They spread out in the jungle, the men separated by as much distance as possible. Each man could see the shape of the man in front of him, but barely. They needed to maintain the separation in case of ambush.

Kinson, convinced they were in Cambodia, wasn't too concerned about an ambush. Charlie, along with everyone else, knew that American forces could not operate in Cambodia. There would be no reason for them to put out ambush patrols. Still, he didn't plan to get sloppy, only that he wasn't worried about an ambush.

That might have been the reason why he walked right into it without a hint of anything wrong. He had halted briefly, one knee on the damp, rotting vegetation, and listened to the quiet rustle of tiny claws. He cocked his head but saw nothing. Then walked forward, bent slightly, as if heading into a strong wind.

There was no warning. Just a sudden sound as though someone had thrown a rock through the trees. Kinson turned toward the sound, realized that no one would be throwing rocks and dived to the right, snapping off the safety on his M-16. He buried his face in his arms and prayed that the grenade would detonate far enough away that he wouldn't be hurt.

The explosion ripped through the jungle. Kinson heard the shrapnel whistle overhead and strike a tree. As it did, he rolled right and looked up. AKs opened fire. Muzzle-flashes winked about waist high. There was a single piercing scream.

Kinson grabbed a grenade, ripped the pin from it and threw it as best he could. Lying on his stomach, afraid to rise up too high, he couldn't put much into the throw. As he released it, he dropped flat.

A machine gun began to hammer. Green tracers flashed over, looking like glowing basketballs. There was an explosion to the side, a fountain of golden sparks and fire. The machine gun stopped shooting and then started again.

M-16s opened up. A half dozen of them, the muzzle-flashes strobing, lighting the trail and the jungle around them. Kinson could see his men, those who still lived, shooting. He could see the bushes and the trees, and occasionally, the enemy.

Now there was shouting. Orders in Vietnamese. Kinson rolled to the right and hit a tall tree. He scrambled around behind it and pulled a second grenade. His rifle would give away his position, but he could toss grenades all night without anyone spotting him.

He yanked the pin free and peeked around the tree. The jungle sparkled and flashed as the VC fired. He aimed at the middle of the enemy lines, threw his grenades and then dropped behind the tree for protection.

The sweat was heavy on him now. He raised his weapon near his eyes as if to inspect it, the rattling of rifles increasing around him. There were poppings from grenades. First Chicom and then American.

"I'm pinned down!"

Kinson recognized the voice. Burgess.

"Hit!" yelled another. A softer voice.

Kinson thought it might have been Tideman. Or maybe one of the Cambodes.

"Count off," he called.

No one answered him. The machine gun hidden in the enemy ambush fired at him. Bullets slammed into the tree. He heard them hitting it. Felt the vibrations.

"Hurtz, can you take the machine gun?"

"Hurtz is down," shouted Burgess.

"Get it," snapped Kinson. As he spoke, he crouched and opened fire with his M-16, burning through the magazine. The last three rounds were tracer, telling him that the magazine was almost empty.

As the bolt locked back, Kinson flattened against the tree and jerked the empty magazine from the weapon. He crouched as the jungle around him seemed to be ripped to pieces. Bits of bark, leaf and wood rained down as the RPD hammered at the tree.

Kinson reached up, touched his last grenade. He jerked it free and yelled, "Use your grenades."

He pulled the pin and threw his at the muzzle-flashes no more than fifteen, twenty yards away. He ducked back, counted and heard the single detonation of the grenade. Just one.

He listened to the sounds of the firing. An RPD hammering away, ripping at the jungle. AKs, ten or twelve of them. All firing on full-auto. But no more M-16s. None.

Kinson wiped his face with his hand. He blinked rapidly, sweat stinging his eyes. There was shouting, but it was all Vietnamese.

Kinson dropped to his knees and then to his belly. He crawled to the right, away from the ambush. He heard the bullets snapping through the air over his head.

The firing from the enemy line slowly tapered. He heard more shouting and knew that they were moving out of hiding to sweep the field. They would rob the dead and probably kill any wounded they found. He would be shot in the back of the head if he didn't get clear.

Reaching out, he touched a body. He felt a wetness on the chest. There was no motion. No sound. A dead man. A dead friend. Kinson crawled closer and saw that it was the body of one of the Cambodes. Killed in the ambush.

Behind him there was more noise. A single shot, and he pictured the VC shooting a wounded man. Then there was a shout. A whoop of triumph. The VC had won. Quickly.

Kinson continued to crawl away from the ambush, thinking only of getting clear. He didn't want to rush. Couldn't rush. He had to take it slowly, quietly, and hope that the enemy would be slow in putting out security and expanding their search area.

There was a shout and a voice near him. He froze, listening, but the man turned and walked away. There was more shouting and another shot.

Kinson started to move again, thinking about the men behind him. His men. They had walked right into the ambush and had never even suspected it. There hadn't been a clue the VC were waiting for them.

But now wasn't the time to worry about that. He had to get out. He stopped, wiped his face and then started off again. The sounds of the enemy were fading in the rear.

MAXWELL HAD RETURNED from the radio room twenty minutes earlier. Kinson and his boys had missed a check-in. Nothing to concern himself about yet. Working with Gerber and the Special Forces, Maxwell knew that sometimes things happened in the field that prevented the radio checks from being made. Sometimes they were too close to the enemy. Sometimes the equipment didn't work. Sometimes the ionosphere didn't cooperate.

Maxwell sat there and looked at the map of South Vietnam he had spread on his desk. Nui Ba Den was more or less in the way, but then there was a Special Forces radio relay station on the top of the mountain to help pass radio traffic.

He stood up and walked around, trying to figure out why he was bothered by the lack of a radio contact. He stopped in front of the safe, touched the lock, but didn't open it. There was nothing in there that would help.

When he sat down again and put his feet up on the desk, a knock sounded on the door, and he turned toward it. "Come," he shouted.

"You through for the day?" asked Reed, sticking his head just inside.

Maxwell stretched his hands high over his head. "It's not going well," he said, ignoring Reed's question.

Reed entered and closed the door. "What happened?"

Maxwell laughed. A single short bark. "Nothing happened. Something didn't happen. No radio check."

"But that's no problem."

"No, supposedly not," Maxwell said. "I have a gut feeling about this. I don't like it. We had a simple mission that shouldn't have presented us with a problem. Simple radio checks and now they've missed one."

Reed shrugged. "Happens all the time."

"Christ," said Maxwell, "you've learned all about it already. Well, I'm uneasy about this. I think something's wrong."

"So what are you going to do?"

"That's the question, isn't it?"

Reed nodded and then asked, "You going to hang around here much longer?"

"Nice try, Reed. I'm not a fool. What you really want to know is if you can go home now."

"Okay," said Reed. "Can I?"

Maxwell waved a hand. "Go."

Reed started to move and then stopped. "You didn't answer the real question. What are you going to do?"

"I'll think of something," he said. "You're not going to stay and listen to all my ideas, are you?"

"I can take a hint," said Reed. He opened the door and disappeared.

Maxwell looked up at the ceiling and wondered just what he should do. Gerber and Fetterman were around Saigon, and they could get into the field pretty quickly. Fetterman would be able to find the patrol, probably in a matter of hours. He'd have an answer.

But then, what if nothing was wrong except that the radio was down for that check-in? An equipment failure and he starts jumping through hoops.

It was the leak, or rather the suspicion of a leak. Maxwell was sure that someone was talking out of turn and giving the enemy valuable information.

MACV had always been a sieve. People in and out with more information than they should have. But now someone seemed to be channeling it to people who shouldn't get it. That was why he was so worried about the patrol. Not that they had missed a radio check but because they were out there and someone might have said something.

There was nothing he could do at the moment, anyway. If he waited until morning, the situation might resolve itself. Or there might be more information available. And if something had gone horribly wrong, there was nothing he could do, even if he moved immediately. Even if he knew where to go and what to take with him.

Maxwell stood up and moved to the door. Things would have to wait until the morning. He turned off the lights, locked the door and headed down the hall to the iron gate.

6

NEAR THE CAMBODIAN
BORDER

Kinson wasn't sure that he was happy to see the sun. He could travel faster in the light, but then the enemy could find him easier. They could spot his trail, though for the last couple of hours, he had tried to leave no sign. They could get to the high ground, or climb a tree and search for movement a hundred or two hundred or even a thousand yards in the distance. The sun might not be his friend.

He stopped at the edge of a ravine, knelt on the wet carpeting of rotting leaves and dead plants and rested. Sweat soaked his uniform and dripped from his face. The jungle on the other side of the ravine looked like a green wall. Fog drifted through it. A light, white fog that looked like smoke from a wood fire.

He wiped the sweat from his face with the sleeve of his uniform, then looked down into the ravine. It was no more than ten feet deep, but the side was steep and he wouldn't be able to climb down without leaving signs.

He got to his feet and moved to the south, along the edge of the ravine. He moved in and out of the thick trees, walking slowly, carefully, not wanting to leave the smallest sign. He would provide the VC with nothing—if they knew that he had escaped the ambush.

The jungle around him came alive. Monkeys screamed in the tops of the trees. Birds took off squawking and landed again, still squawking. Lizards, sluggish with the chill of the morning, scurried up the trunks of trees. Insects buzzed. The sound swelled around him, hiding the noise he was making as he hurried back toward South Vietnam. But also hiding the sound of the enemy.

The ravine flattened out and he hurried across it, up the gentle slope of the other side and then deeper into the jungle. He listened for human sounds. The distant crash of artillery and the rumble of high-flying jets. If he could get into South Vietnam, he could get picked up by a helicopter.

Again he stopped, in the shadow of a giant teak tree. Tucked in against the smooth bark, hidden in the folds of the tree and the blackness where the sun couldn't penetrate, he pulled out his canteen, drinking from it greedily. Water dribbled down his chin to soak the collar of his fatigue shirt. He knew he was wasting water, drinking too much of it too fast, but he couldn't help himself.

In survival school he had been told that the first things pilots did after a crash or after bailout was drink all their water. If they were near a stream or a pond, they'd drink from that, not worried about disease. Kinson hadn't worried about that because he didn't think he'd ever be in an aircraft accident. What he hadn't understood then was that the stress of the situation made the survivor thirsty. Having fled an ambush was the same as having crashed a jet.

He wiped his mouth and swirled the canteen around. There was some water in the bottom, but not very much. He'd already drained one canteen. He shrugged and finished it off, then put the empty container away. He didn't want to leave it behind, because Charlie would find it and use it. No point in making it a gift to the enemy.

Sunlight began to invade the jungle, filtering through the holes in the canopy. The shafts of light made the jungle look almost holy as they lanced the ground, shining on the plants and bushes, making them glow a bright green. Water dripped, setting a quiet rhythm in the background. It filled the big leaves, which eventually tipped over, spilling the water to the jungle floor with a loud noise. The sporadic sounds sent animals scurrying, and forced Kinson's heart to race.

He worked his way to the east, not worrying about the map or exactly where he was. When he entered South Vietnam he'd know it. He'd be able to see aircraft to the east. There would be activity in South Vietnam that wouldn't be happening in Cambodia. He might have to walk a klick or two into South Vietnam before he knew he was there, but eventually he'd know it.

Again he stopped. The undergrowth was beginning to get thick. Wait-a-minute vines tore at his shirt. Bushes and branches of small trees filled the space around him. The broad leaves of the bushes and the thin, spidery leaves of ferns were all around. He couldn't see more than a yard in any direction.

He crouched, remembering his survival training. Travel at night or in the worst possible weather. Never take a road or use a stream unless trying to avoid dogs. Stick to the roughest terrain and hole up in the day. Never use a haystack, a barn or a cave because the enemy would look there first. Hide in thick undergrowth with more than one way out.

He got down on his belly and wiggled deeper into the undergrowth. He found a patch of sunlight and thought that it might dry his feet. He couldn't take off his boots, but he could wrap himself around the thick trunk of a bush, the branches hanging down to hide him, and stick his feet into the bit of sun. For a few minutes anyway.

When he laid down he did not remove his equipment, knowing that if something happened to force him from hiding, he'd forget anything not attached to him. He loosened the sling of his rifle and wrapped it around his hand. Finally comfortable, he relaxed and listened to the sounds around him. Nothing to suggest the enemy was coming at him.

He knew that he wouldn't be able to sleep. Not with everything that had happened during the night, but he did have to rest. Besides, he should lay holed up for the day anyway. The next night he would start off again and, with luck, be picked up in the morning. It would take only the slightest luck.

Then, before he knew it, he was asleep.

GERBER WOKE TO THE SOUND of someone pounding on his door. He had been dreaming of artillery and mortar fire, and at first the crashing from the door had been incorporated into the dreams. Then suddenly he snapped awake, but the sound didn't stop.

He rolled over and looked at the door, wishing that whoever it was would go away. He got up and walked over, leaning close. "Yeah."

"Captain?"

Gerber unlocked it, then turned and walked away so that Fetterman would have to let himself in. He headed for the bed, rubbing a hand through his hair.

Morrow had rolled over on her back and was staring up at the ceiling.

Fetterman entered. "Morning, Captain. Robin. Sorry to intrude."

Gerber sat on the edge of the bed, staring down at the floor. Without looking up he said, "I'm not ready for this. Not one bit."

"Sorry to break in, Captain," said Fetterman. He glanced at Robin who had pulled the sheet up to her chin, but that did little to conceal the shape of her body under the light fabric. He pulled his eyes away and turned back to Gerber. "I know you told me not to talk to anyone at MACV and to hide so they couldn't find me . . ."

"Christ, Tony, what time is it?"

"After seven."

"You say that as if I should be ashamed of myself for having the audacity to stay in bed until after seven."

"No, sir. It's just that the world is up and the war is still on."

Gerber stood up, waved at him without looking, and padded into the bathroom. Water ran and Gerber returned with a glass.

"You could have gotten me some, too," said Morrow.

Gerber handed her the glass and retreated. He reappeared and then walked over to the chair, sat down and took a drink. "All right, Tony, what you got?"

He glanced at Morrow.

"Come on, Tony. She already knows more secrets about us than the CIA. She's trustworthy."

"Yes, sir. Maxwell's worried about a patrol that failed to check in last night at midnight. Missed a second check at six this morning."

"So, what's the point?"

"Maxwell would like us to hit the field in search of those troops."

"Shit," said Gerber. "Any details?"

"Briefing is to be held at eight. Gives us a little less than an hour to get there."

"And no time to eat breakfast."

"No, sir."

Robin said, "You don't seem to be worried about some missing people."

"Hell, Robin, I've been on enough of these boondoggles where the radio communications were less than perfect that I never worry about it. Not unless there's another reason to worry."

"I'll meet you in the lobby," said Fetterman.

Gerber finished the water and set the glass down. Again he rubbed his face, using both hands. He yawned and said, "I'll be down in fifteen minutes."

"Yes, sir. I'll let myself out."

When the door closed, Morrow said, "You know, I should follow up on this. A lost American squad on a mission for the CIA."

Gerber sat back in the chair and stared at her. "I don't believe that Sergeant Fetterman mentioned a missing American squad that was a CIA operation."

She sat up, letting the sheet drop away. "He didn't have to. He said Maxwell and that means CIA. I doubt that Maxwell would call you in if it wasn't Americans, so it means an American patrol. Simple."

"Simple," repeated Gerber. "I'm going to shower."

"You mind if I join you?"

Gerber stopped at the door and looked at her. "I've only got fifteen minutes."

"Yeah, you didn't think ahead on that, did you?"

"No, really."

Fifteen minutes later Gerber, wearing clean jungle fatigues, found Fetterman sitting in the lobby reading the *Stars and Stripes*. "Says in the paper here that the Marines up in Quang Nam killed about three thousand VC and NVA."

Gerber stared and then said, "I don't know why I read the paper."

"You already heard this?" asked Fetterman.

"No, and now I don't have to read about it, either."

"Sorry I barged in on you, Captain," said Fetterman suddenly. "I didn't think Robin would mind."

Gerber laughed. "No, she didn't mind. I mind. I needed another thirty minutes."

"Ah," said Fetterman, understanding. "Well, I've arranged for a taxi to pick us up. Should be waiting outside."

They left the hotel, stepping out into the muggy heat of the morning. The taxi driver, a small dark man in a flowered shirt and fatigue pants, stood holding half a five-dollar bill. When he saw Fetterman, he waved it like a banner, afraid that Fetterman would catch a ride with someone else.

"Promised him that I would pay him five dollars American if he'd wait."

"And then gave him half the bill as incentive."

"Exactly."

They climbed into the rear of the cab. It wasn't a mess like the one they had used a couple of days before. Sometime in the past month the driver had swept it. And he had attended a driving school. No kamikaze tactics on the road. He waited for others to make their moves and dodged them, filling the holes they had created. It didn't take him long to get them to MACV Headquarters.

When they arrived, Fetterman gave him the other half of the five and the man was happy. No argument about the fee. He wanted the greenbacks, which were more valuable than the Monopoly money that GIs usually used.

As they walked up to the front door, Gerber asked, "You really don't know any more about this?"

"No, sir. Since the line wasn't secure, we had to talk in riddles."

They walked down the hall, descended the steps and stopped in front of the iron gate. The MP there recognized Gerber and had him sign in. Fetterman followed suit and they were admitted. They walked on down to Maxwell's office and Gerber knocked on the door.

"Come."

Gerber opened the door and entered, flopping down on the visitor's chair. Fetterman moved to the file cabinets and leaned against them while Maxwell, sitting at his desk, picked up a Coke can, shook it and then set it down.

"Morning, Jerry," said Gerber. "You got us up pretty damned early for this."

Maxwell turned to face them. There were dark circles under his eyes, and his face was pasty, sick-looking. There was a pallor to his skin tone.

"What's going on, Jerry?" asked Gerber.

"I've got a squad out in the field and they've missed two checks."

"We missed checks, too."

Maxwell leaned closer, glanced at Fetterman and said, "I've a bad feeling about this. I think they've stepped into some shit."

"Any reason for that?"

"Things haven't been going well for the past few weeks. Too much of our information has been getting passed around to too many people."

Gerber shook his head. "Jerry, this is the first I've heard of any of this."

"Look," said Maxwell, "I might be talking out of school, but you can't keep anything quiet here. I've got to coordinate everything through so many different levels of command and bureaucracy and then coordinate it with the Vietnamese, that it's a wonder we ever get anything accomplished without the whole world knowing about it."

"That's a problem we've all had since we got here," said Fetterman. "What makes things different now?"

Maxwell shrugged. "That's just it. Maybe there's nothing going on. But I just think someone new is letting out all our secrets."

Gerber was quiet for a moment. "What do you want us to do about it?"

"I'd like you two to hit the field and see if you can't find this squad. I can give you the LZ they used and their destination. Maybe you could find out what happened to them."

Fetterman frowned. "I don't know, Jerry."

"Pick up some help from the SOG people," said Maxwell as if he hadn't heard what Fetterman said, "and spend a day or so searching. It should be a fairly easy task."

"When are they supposed to check in again?"

"If they missed at six, which they did, they are supposed to try again two hours later. If they missed that, then every hour on the hour."

"And you've heard nothing."

"Not a word. It's almost as if they jumped into a void. Chopper pilots got them in and reported no enemy movement and no fire taken. Once they moved into the jungle, they vanished."

Fetterman turned so that he could lean against the wall. "If there's a leak, then we're going to have our butts hanging out, too."

"No," said Maxwell. "No one is going to know about this but you and me."

Gerber laughed. "You've cleared this with no one?"

"No one."

"Then our butts are going to be hanging out even farther."

"All I want," said Maxwell, "is to find out what happened to my troops."

"Jerry, you tried this on us once before. We were out looking for some men you'd lost."

"This is different, Mack," said Maxwell. "That was a CIA unit that walked into an ambush. We knew what happened to them. But these are Army men. Your people. And we don't have a clue about what happened to them."

"Tony?"

"Shit, Captain, how can we refuse? No one's ordering us out, and Jerry here is telling us they are Army. We've got to go take a look."

"Who else is going to know about this?" asked Gerber.

"Like I told you, no one but you and me and the men you take. I don't want anything else to happen."

Gerber looked at his watch. "We can get airlifted in by noon. Gives us three hours to get ready." He glanced at Fetterman. "Overnight?"

"Sure, Captain. I can get us four guys over at SOG. Top men to go with us."

"How about just two others?" suggested Gerber.

"Whatever, Captain."

"We'll do it, Jerry," said Gerber.

"Mack, I might be all wet about this. It might just be bad luck or something like that. But I'm taking no chances until I learn some more about what is going on. I have a feeling in my gut that I just can't ignore."

Gerber got up. "Tan Son Nhut at noon?"

"I'll start making the arrangements now and have a chopper there for you."

"You'd better meet us at SOG about eleven with a briefing on what's going on out there."

"No problem."

Gerber moved to the door and opened it. As he did, Reed stumbled in. He glanced at Gerber and then Fetterman and said, "Good morning."

Gerber ignored him and said, "Eleven, Jerry."

"Right."

Gerber stepped into the hall and Fetterman closed the door behind him.

"What was that all about?" asked Reed.

Maxwell turned to his desk and picked up a file folder. He shrugged and said, "Nothing much."

Reed looked at the CIA man and then at the door. "Those guys were Special Forces."

"How do you know?"

"Christ, Jerry, give me some credit for having eyes. I saw them, and they all wear those damned patches, those jump wings and carry those silly hats. I'd have to be stupid not to know they were Special Forces."

Maxwell laughed. "Yeah."

"So, you sending them out to look for the missing patrol?" he asked.

"How do you know the patrol is still missing?"

"What the hell is this, an inquisition? I stopped by the radio room and checked on it. No message traffic from the squad. Therefore they haven't reported and are still missing. Therefore you've called some of your Special Forces buddies to go out and look for those soldiers."

"That doesn't go beyond this room," said Maxwell.

"Of course not," said Reed. He dropped into the visitor's chair and asked, "What's on tap for today?"

Maxwell shook his head. "We've got a briefing for the commander at one o'clock. I thought you might like to handle that one."

"What's he looking for?"

Maxwell lowered his voice and tried to modulate it like the newscasters on the radio or the nightly television newscasts. "Vietcong sappers dropped mortars into our camp at Nha Trang. Four rounds exploded harmlessly. Damage was light and countermortar was successful."

"You're kidding?"

"Nope. Just a roundup of what happened last night and early this morning. Any new reports of the enemy activity. If you spot a trend, you mention it. Illustrate it with slides and you'll have it knocked."

Reed glanced at his watch. "I skipped breakfast this morning so that I could get in here on time. I might go find something to eat now and then skip lunch so that I can be ready for the briefing at one."

"Whatever," said Maxwell.

Reed stood up. "I'll be ready at one."

"You know where to find the information for the briefing?" Maxwell stared at the younger man.

"Third drawer of the safe. And check the message traffic for the past twelve hours."

"Right. Have one of the Spec Fours mark it for you, and then use the best of it. A general view of the war, going into specifics in the large, more important incidents if there were any."

"Got it," said Reed. "I'll be back in what, an hour or so?"

Maxwell nodded. "Don't take much more than an hour. I may not be here when you return."

"I've got it covered," said Reed. "Catch you later." He opened the door and stepped into the hallway. Things were beginning to move quickly. Faster than he had expected.

7

THE OUTSKIRTS
OF SAIGON

Reed lay back against the wall and looked at the sweat-coated highlights of Thi's naked body. She lay partially on him, her head nestled on his stomach. With one hand, she tickled the inside of his thigh, watching his response. Finally he reached out and touched her bare bottom. He drew his fingers toward him, over the curve of her spine.

"You have not eaten, yet," she said, her breath warm against his body.

"Sure I have." He smiled broadly and moved his hand to her shoulder.

"I meant food."

"I'm not hungry. Besides, I don't have time. I have to get back to work."

"Why?" she asked. "You do not have to do anything."

"Ah, but today I do. I must prepare the briefing for the general. This is the first chance I've had to brief the commander. It's very important."

Thi scrambled around and sat on the bed with her legs crossed under her Indian fashion. It was a position that she had learned from Reed.

He studied her body. The small high breasts. The taut skin of her belly. The soft smooth skin of her thighs and the sparse dark triangle of hair. Never had a woman turned him on as she did. He'd give almost anything to stay with her. At least for a while.

"You must brief the general?" she asked, almost in awe.

"Only because my boss is going to be out of the office helping get a patrol ready. One to search for the first that is missing."

"But you will be briefing the general. He will see just how intelligent you are."

Reed laughed at her innocence. "I'm afraid it's not going to be that big a deal. It's a job anyone could do. I just happen to have the opportunity to do it."

She touched him gently, felt his immediate response, and smiled. "But I am so proud."

"And I am so sore."

"You should not talk like that."

Reed shook his head and then slipped to the right and swung his feet to the floor. "If I don't get going, I won't get the briefing done and there'll be nothing to be proud of."

"Then I shall go away, where you will not see me until I have dressed."

"No," said Reed. "That's not necessary. I'll resist the temptation."

"Tonight," she said, shaking her head and her hair, "I will serve you a dinner in celebration." She used her fingers to comb her hair back over her shoulders so that it no longer concealed her nudity.

"Will we eat it naked?" asked Reed.

"Of course not. You would not eat the food then."

"Good point." He picked up his clothes and carried them into the bathroom. He washed himself quickly and then dressed. He used her brush to comb his hair, brushed his teeth with a wet finger and returned to the bedroom.

She sat where he had left her, still naked. "I've got to go," he said.

She got up and walked to him. She tilted her head to be kissed and then took his hand. "Come. I will walk you to the front door."

They descended the stairs together. She held his hand and turned to face him, letting him see everything. He reached out and touched a nipple, felt it respond to his finger, and wished that Maxwell had stayed around to brief the general himself.

"I better go now," he said, "because if I stay much longer, I'm never going to go."

"You just think of me naked while you brief the general," she said.

"I'm afraid that's exactly what I'll do."

With that he opened the door. He hurried toward his jeep parked on the side of the street and surrounded by a dozen children. When they saw him they swarmed forward, their hands out as they screamed for money, candy or cigarettes.

He turned and looked around once and saw the door close slowly. He knew that she was leaning with her back against it. He knew that she was hoping he would return, but that wouldn't work. He had to get to MACV to prepare for the briefing or he'd lose his position.

As he climbed into the driver's seat of the jeep, he thought he saw movement behind one of the upstairs windows. What he didn't know was that she was upstairs scrambling into her clothes because she needed to make her report.

MAXWELL MET GERBER and Fetterman at the SOG building at Tan Son Nhut. It was a low structure with a tin roof and wooden-slat-and-screen sides. A few rooms were completely sealed. They contained small air-conditioning units purchased at the World's Largest PX. In the rear was a warehouse, also completely sealed, that held a stock of supplies and equipment manufactured around the world. A Spike Team could be outfitted for any of the various missions it might be required to run.

Maxwell, wearing his ever-present white suit, wilted white shirt, and tie pulled loose, drove up in a jeep. He shut off the engine and sat there for a moment as the sweat blossomed on his forehead and under his arms. He took out an oversize handkerchief and wiped the moisture from his face. He blinked in the bright tropical sun and finally forced himself out of the jeep.

Inside he was stopped by a big man wearing jungle pants, yellow shower shoes and nothing else. "You can't come in here, sir."

"I'm Maxwell. Here to see Captain Gerber."

"Ah. Follow me, then." He turned and walked along the hallway. The dimly lit corridor smelled of mildew and sweat. He stopped near a door and pointed. "In there."

"Thanks." Maxwell opened the door and found Gerber sitting in a chair at the head of a table, eating cereal.

Gerber waved his spoon in greeting. "Hi, Jerry."

Fetterman was sitting on a couch against the wall, reading a magazine. There were two other men Maxwell didn't recognize. A black man who looked uncomfortably hot even in the air-conditioned room, and a small white man who had light hair and a bad sunburn.

"You ready?" asked Maxwell.

"Anytime." Gerber set his bowl on the table and swallowed. "What you got?"

"I need a map."

Fetterman got up and spread one on the table. The other two men moved closer so that they could see.

"Who you got with you?" asked Maxwell.

"Leon McCarthy, late of the Army Rangers but now sufficiently trained to be Special Forces, and Bruce Hoffs, a newcomer to our climate, which explains his sunburn."

McCarthy asked, "Who's this?"

Fetterman smiled. "We're not supposed to know. His identity and job are a secret, but we believe he's Jerry Maxwell of the CIA."

"Funny," said Maxwell. "Now, if you've a few minutes to be serious..."

"Go ahead, Jerry," said Gerber.

"Not much to tell you now. They've failed to make every radio check, including the emergency checks in the last hour. Naturally we've failed to raise them."

"Could be they're sitting right in the middle of an enemy company and have to lie low until the enemy moves away," offered Fetterman.

Maxwell shot him a glance and shook his head. "I'd feel better if we checked this out."

"Sure."

Maxwell pointed at the map, at a portion northwest of Tay Ninh City and west of Nui Ba Den. Jungle—a few streams and one open area that was swamp—and no rice paddies.

"We put them in here, to cross into Cambodia and head for Kampong Trach, here. A sneak-and-peek operation. See if the enemy was building up in the vicinity. Nothing too elaborate. Avoid contact."

"What LZ did they use?"

Maxwell pointed again. "In here. Got the coordinates from the pilot. He'll be taking you out there today so you'll hit the same LZ. Then it's up to you."

Fetterman wiped a hand over his face. "Militarily it doesn't make good sense to use the same LZ. Charlie could be waiting for us there."

"That's up to you," said Maxwell. "If you want to use another LZ and then try to find the trail, go ahead. I've given you the jump-off point and the destination."

"What can you tell us about their itinerary?" asked Gerber.

"They were going to cross the border at night, so they moved slowly during the day. That's about it."

Gerber looked at Fetterman. "Tony?"

"I'd feel more comfortable if we gave them a chance to report in. We might walk up on them and compromise them. I sure as hell wouldn't want some hot dog from Saigon fucking up my mission when I had everything under control."

Maxwell pulled out one of the chairs and sat down in it. He glanced at Fetterman and then back at the map. "I don't think we've got that problem. I've a gut feeling."

"You keep saying that, Jerry," said Gerber. "I'd feel better with something more concrete. Now, anything else?"

"Chopper'll be at Hotel Three at noon, as requested," said Maxwell.

"Anyone have any questions?" Gerber looked at each of the men, and when there was no response, said, "I think that's got it, Jerry."

Maxwell stood up. "What about check-in?"

Fetterman said, "Not with your boys. Not if you think you've got leaks..."

"Sergeant Fetterman!" snapped Maxwell, nodding toward the two new men.

"Jerry, these guys are going out into the field with us, they have the right to know what's going on around them. Besides, they're trustworthy."

Maxwell shrugged then. "I don't like everyone knowing my business."

"It's not just your business, Jerry," said Gerber. "If you can ask men to risk their lives, you can let them know why it has to be done."

"Okay. Okay." Maxwell held up his hands.

"If there's nothing else," said Gerber, "we'll get ready to hit the field."

"That's all I have for now," said Maxwell.

"You going to be at Hotel Three?" asked Fetterman.

"I think it'll be better if I avoid that. Let the competition wonder just what the hell is going on. I'll hang around here, though, if no one objects."

Gerber smiled. "Hell, Jerry, you can go with us, if that makes you feel any better."

THE QUIET RUSTLING woke Kinson. He snapped awake, his eyes flying open, but he didn't move. He felt his ears move, like radar dishes, trying to focus on the noise, afraid that it was a snake crawling toward him. And then he was afraid it wasn't. He could easily defeat a snake. Then he heard a voice, quiet, the words lost on the light breeze. The creatures walking through the jungle were human.

Slowly Kinson took inventory. He could feel his pack, canteens, first aid kit and pistol belt pressing into his body. His rifle sling was still wrapped around his hand, which now ached from the tightness of the sling. But he didn't dare move. That was death in the jungle.

He was soaked in sweat. It was funny. He had gone to sleep fairly dry, even after his march through the nighttime jungle, and now he was wringing wet. It was almost as if sleeping was such hard work that he sweated from all the activity. But he knew he hadn't moved in his sleep. He was in the same position, facing the same spine-covered trunk of the bush that hid him when he'd gone to sleep.

He closed his eyes, listened, and then was overwhelmed by the odor. Rotting vegetation, the pungent scent of the bright flowers and the stench of something that had died and hadn't been picked apart by scavengers. Heat, humidity and now a rotting body.

And insects. He could hear them buzzing, some of them close and some of them in the distance. The insistent sounds suddenly grated on his nerves. One of them darted close to his ear, sending chills down his spine, but Kinson didn't move and didn't swat at it.

The voices came to him again. A quiet buzz barely audible above the rustling of the breeze through the trees, but not loud enough for him to pick out words. There were people close, but he didn't know whose people. The safest thing was to stay where he was, frozen against the trunk of the bush, hidden until he learned if they were Americans.

Kinson turned his head slightly, looking into the shadows that played across the jungle floor. There was a flash of color, but it was a bird diving in. There was a quiet rattling of a bush as a lizard climbed it, and to the right, a spray of gray. A spider's web caught in the light.

But there was nothing human around him. It was as if he were lost in a Mesozoic world, where animals ruled and the human race was still a hundred million years in the future.

Then the voices came again, but now he could pick out words. Vietnamese. Maybe a South Vietnamese patrol, but more likely the Vietcong. Now he was glad that he hadn't moved out when he heard them.

He closed his eyes, resting his head on the ground. He listened as the rustling in the bushes came closer, and he wondered if it was a snake or his imagination. The sound of the voices drew near and he wondered if they were searching for him. They seemed to be too calm to be part of a search party. Searchers would move silently, hoping to catch him off guard.

This had to be a normal patrol, looking for signs that the Americans had been in the area. Kinson wouldn't move, almost didn't dare to breathe.

And as he lay there, his back began to itch. First had come the sounds of something moving through the brush toward him, and then he was sure he could feel something rubbing up against him. The skin on the back of his neck crawled as he waited for the beast, the snake, the lizard, to sink its teeth into his flesh.

But he refused to move. The sweat trickled, tickling him, and the skin on his back seemed to be on fire, but he refused to move. Any motion could be seen, no matter how slow, and he knew the enemy was out there, not far from him.

His whole body revolted then. He wanted a drink of water, the thirst suddenly overwhelming. His shoulder, hips and legs ached with the enforced immobility. His bladder seemed ready to burst, and his guts suddenly cramped.

Still he refused to move. He listened as the Vietnamese voices faded and the last rattle of equipment disappeared. Again the jungle was silent, or rather, was without human sound. There were insects buzzing, the quiet drip of water and the calls of the animals.

Kinson told himself that the enemy was gone. He convinced himself that slight movement would not betray him. He reached down with one hand and unfastened his fly. He began to urinate, a slow, almost painful process as he restricted the flow so that there was no noise. A quiet feeble stream, and after an eternity he felt his belly loosen and his bladder relax. One source of discomfort was gone.

He rolled onto his back and wiggled slightly, carefully, and the itching vanished. Now he lay flat and the pain in his body faded away. Finally he opened his third canteen and took a small drink.

Lying there, staring up into the canopy, he felt better. He could see the dark underside of the foliage. A monkey ran across it, launched itself into space and caught another branch, flipping itself up into the thin vegetation and vanishing among the leaves.

It was midday, but Kinson wasn't hungry. He wasn't tired. He wanted to get the hell out of there but knew that could mean death. The enemy was out there searching for him, and since he was alone, the only thing he could do was stay hidden until he could move safely. That would be after dark.

He slipped away from the puddle he had created, rolled to his side and concentrated on the last football game he had seen. He worked at bringing it into sharp focus, reliving everything from the opening kickoff to the final gun. It wasn't that spectacular a game, but it did occupy his mind, and that was the whole purpose. Fifteen minutes later he was asleep again.

FETTERMAN ENTERED the jungle at the point he thought the first patrol had used. As they had flown in, Fetterman had been crouching between the pilot's seats, studying the terrain in front of them. He thought he could detect a slight discoloration of the grass, as if someone had moved through it a day or two earlier. The paths seemed to converge at a point on the western side of the LZ.

As soon as the chopper had landed, Fetterman had been out, moving forward. He ducked beneath the rotors and ran toward the jungle. He stopped short and crouched, studying the ground around him.

The single helicopter lifted, hovered in a cloud of dust and loose grass and then took off. It climbed over the trees and then leveled off to the north. The roar of the turbine and the popping of the blades faded rapidly, and they were left in silence.

Gerber, with Hoffs and McCarthy, followed about ten yards behind. Fetterman glanced at them once, pointed to the right and left and then moved forward into the trees.

Gerber caught him there and Fetterman indicated the ground. "They regrouped here," he whispered. "Took some time about it, and then moved off in that direction."

"You sure?"

"Fairly positive," said Fetterman. "You can see points where the men rested. Grass and vegetation beaten down a little more than that surrounding it."

"Then let's get going," said Gerber.

Fetterman followed the trail blazed by the first squad. He moved carefully, keeping his eyes on the ground in front of him, but also looking for booby traps. He doubted he'd find any. The first squad would have tripped them if there were any. And if that happened, there would be evidence of it.

He moved for ten minutes and then stopped. Behind him
Gerber and the other two men spread out in a rough circle for
security. Each man listened for sounds of the enemy. They
were making sure that the enemy hadn't found and were following them.

After the brief rest, Fetterman was up again. Slipping
through the thick vegetation, he stepped carefully so that he
didn't leave any sign. He ducked under low-hanging branches
and lifted his feet over small trees struggling to push up
through the thick carpet of decaying vegetation. He tried not
to scuff his feet. He set them down toe first, rolling his foot to
the rear. A long, involved, tiring process that left the carpet
undisturbed and gave him a chance to react if he found a trip-
wire and a pressure plate.

He kept going for fifteen minutes and then took another rest.
He listened to the noise around him. The animals and birds
didn't seem to be concerned. They were moving around as if
nothing were out of place. Fetterman knew that large patrols
of sloppy men caused the animals to flee, but a small, intelligent patrol of soldiers who knew what they were doing could
slide through the jungle without disturbing the animals.

They started again, heading along the trail. Fetterman
veered off, paralleling it now. He would cross over to it, but
now that the jungle was thicker, he could see the path taken
by the others. They might have thought they were moving like
a fog, but they had left signs enough for anyone who knew
what to look for.

After a few minutes Fetterman halted again, and Gerber
approached him.

"They stayed here quite a while," he whispered. He pointed
at the spots where the vegetation was crushed and the jungle
carpet disturbed. "Not much evidence, but enough."

Gerber glanced upward toward the canopy but couldn't see
the sky. He then checked the time. "About seven hours to
sunset."

"No problem, Captain."

Fetterman started out again. He skirted the huge trunk of a teak tree and slipped between two palms. He walked slowly, eyes on the ground, the trees and then the canopy. He now knew that he only had to follow a compass course. The other squad hadn't varied from a straight path once they had gotten away from the LZ. Now he could look for signs that they had been followed, but the only indications were from the American patrol. No one else had been in there for a good two or three weeks. The jungle quickly hid any signs.

For two hours they continued on, stopping and starting, listening to everything around them. They slipped along through dark patches, avoiding the areas of brightness. The heat and humidity wrapped them like a wet blanket in a steam bath. Their uniforms were soaked and blackened by their sweat. Each of them pretended that he was unaffected by the environment, but even men in top condition found the jungle hard to take. It sapped their strength, turning them weak in a short time.

But Fetterman finally stopped. He glanced right and left and then waved Gerber forward.

"What's the problem?"

"We're there."

"How do you know?"

"Captain, can't you smell it? We've found the missing men."

Gerber took a deep breath and said, "Oh."

8

MACV HEADQUARTERS
SAIGON

Reed sat in Maxwell's office, trying to put together the briefing he had to give. He had spent fifteen minutes organizing the files, papers and documents that Maxwell had spread out earlier, before leaving. There seemed to be no reason or organization to it. Whatever Maxwell had needed was pulled out and then left where it had been when he finished with it. Unless it was classified. Then it was in the safe.

Reed had tried to sort it out, found the task impossible and then just stacked everything, pushing it all to the side, near the line of empty Coke cans. He then sat down, a legal pad in front of him, and the overnight, after-action reports near his right hand.

He sat there for a moment and realized that it was all beginning to fall apart. Maxwell was worried about a leak in MACV, and when they found the missing patrol, Maxwell would be even more convinced that there was a leak.

He rocked back and looked at the cinder block wall. Of course there were so many people privy to the information, it was hard to isolate a single source. In the last few weeks, Maxwell had been limiting the spread of information, slowly trying to reduce the number of people who knew what was going on, in order to eliminate the leak. The obvious problem was the South Vietnamese.

Reed had seen it happen a dozen times before. An American officer would have proof that a South Vietnamese soldier was Vietcong. Definite proof that he would present to the proper authorities, but by the time anyone showed up to arrest the VC man or woman, he or she was gone. Warned by other friends who hadn't been compromised.

There was a story circulating throughout the headquarters about the South Vietnamese man who seemed to be the most loyal of the Vietnamese. He helped without having been asked. He circulated through the building, almost at will, but no one could find one thing in his background to suggest he was anything but loyal. The day after the Tet attacks, his body had been found, an AK in his hand, a chest pouch strapped to him. He had been leading one of the attacks on the air base at Tan Son Nhut.

The task of preparing the briefing was forgotten as Reed concentrated on the puzzle. Where could he *find* a leak?

The Cambodes were an obvious source. Easy to blame them, but anyone who thought about it would realize that they could only be responsible for the one leak. When people started scrambling, looking for a scapegoat, they would surface and the cloud thrown up might be enough to obscure the issue.

He smiled to himself. If someone asked a few hard questions, then there was a man who had a relationship with a Vietnamese. That might be a place to begin an investigation. Men talked to women about their jobs and a man with a loose tongue might accidentally tell a woman everything he knew. More than one spy had been female, taking bedroom talk to the Intelligence headquarters.

Since many of the secrets were kept out of the hands of the South Vietnamese, that seemed to be the place to look. And Gary Pittman was seeing a Vietnamese woman. He had been

with her on many a night. Reed couldn't help grinning as he
thought about it. Pittman was seeing Thi, too. He had been
seeing her for more than six months, and Thi had chased Reed
out of the house once because Pittman had appeared at the
front door. Reed had even had to hide his jeep so that Pittman
wouldn't suspect he'd been seeing Thi.

It made sense. Pittman was privy to everything at MACV
Headquarters. Reed could turn the man in, have him inves-
tigated, and the mere fact that he had been under suspicion was
enough to get him transferred home. His rival for Thi's affec-
tions would be gone.

But then, if he was wrong, he could be the one in trouble.
Someone might learn that the leak was not Pittman. No, decided Reed, the move of the hour was to follow the man himself, build evidence against him and then they'd have to get rid
of him. Later they might learn he was innocent, but by then
it would be too late.

He turned his attention to the after-action reports, reading
through them quickly. Not much action the night before.
Mortars falling on a few camps, and rockets into a couple of
cities. No trends had manifested themselves, so there was
nothing to say along those lines.

The only thing going on was the possibility of another VC
and NVA attack on Saigon. A thousand men, two thousand,
thrown into the city to disrupt services, blow up a few buildings and sacrifice themselves in front of the news cameras so
the people in the United States would think that the VC and
NVA were still a major force.

He took his legal pad, wrote "Secret" at the top, then began to list the incidents from the night before. Now that he had
thought of a solution to his problem, he could concentrate on
the immediate task. He didn't know that he was smiling as he
added in the reports of three Americans who died because a
mortar had fallen on an NCO club in Ban Me Thuot.

GERBER REALIZED immediately what the stench blowing at him meant. Death. There were men lying in the jungle, dead for twelve or fifteen hours, the heat baking the juices from their bodies, the tropical environment accelerating the process of decay. And since the deaths of the men were violent, their bodies ripped open by bullets and shrapnel, exposing the soft interiors, the decay spread even faster.

Gerber reached up and rubbed his nose, but it did no good. "I guess we found them, all right."

Fetterman moved in closer. "I'll check them if you'll handle the security."

"No," said Gerber. "I think we'd better both look at them. McCarthy and Hoffs can take security."

Gerber drew back and found Hoffs facing to the rear. "I think we've found them. You and McCarthy take security for us. Fetterman and I will move in."

"Yes, sir."

Hoffs found McCarthy and the three of them moved toward Fetterman. With Fetterman on the point, they headed deeper into the jungle. Fetterman moved around a bush and found the first of the bodies. It was that of a young man, lying on his face, the back of his uniform riddled with holes. The blood, dried to a rusty brown, had stained it and the ground under him. His helmet was gone, as well as his weapon and his equipment, and there was a single bullet hole in the back of his head.

Gerber moved past the master sergeant and around a bush. He found another corpse, lying on its right side, the knees hiked up and the arms wrapped around its belly. There was a thick pool of blood under him, the surface sticky.

The man's intestines were gathered in his hands as if he were trying to stuff them back into his stomach. He had died trying to keep his body together.

And like the first man all his equipment was gone, as were his boots. Gerber knelt next to him and saw that two of his pockets had been cut open. That meant the enemy had time to search the bodies. It was more than just picking up the equipment, it was a systematic search for intelligence data they might have.

Gerber moved on, found a third man with a single bullet hole in his face. The eyes had bulged out. He apparently had died in the first few minutes of the battle and had fallen out of the way. All of his equipment was gone, too.

Fetterman found one of the Cambodes. Not only had he been killed, but the body had been mutilated. All the fingers were cut off, the eyes were gouged out and his heart was missing. The equipment the man had carried was stacked near him, telling everyone that the man was so despised that no one would steal his gear.

"NVA telling the Cambodians that they won't tolerate anyone assisting the South Vietnamese or the Americans. Mutilations are ritualistic, especially that nonsense with the eyes. Means the spirit wanders because it is blinded," said Fetterman as Gerber approached.

Gerber nodded and moved on. He found the second Cambodian. He too had been mutilated. The enemy hadn't liked them at all. The American bodies showed only the wounds inflicted in the fighting.

Gerber returned, moving back along the line, counting the bodies. There was a snap of a twig and Gerber dropped to one knee. McCarthy appeared. "I think someone's coming up on us."

Gerber turned and looked into the jungle. He heard a noise, equipment rattling. He glanced to the right and saw that Fetterman was crouching, his face turned toward the sound. When the sergeant pointed at it, Gerber nodded and motioned to the rear. Hoffs stood up and moved then, drifting toward the center. They hurried away from the ambush site. Fetterman took the point and then slid to a stop.

When Gerber caught him, Fetterman whispered. "They're in front of us, too."

That made sense. The enemy, if they knew that Gerber and the patrol were there, would want to send out a blocking force. Wouldn't have to be many men, just four or five guys, and who would be able to stop them?

"Captain?"

Gerber nodded. "Head to the south."

McCarthy caught up and said, "They're no more than fifty yards behind us."

"CS and then explosive grenades," said Gerber. "As soon as we get the detonations, we move to the south."

"Got it."

Hoffs appeared, a CS grenade in his hand. "Hoffs, you and McCarthy throw toward the blocking force and Fetterman and I'll hit those chasing us. Then all four throw the explosives at the chasing force."

"Got it."

Gerber took a CS grenade, pulled the pin and then nodded. As he did, he came up and threw the gas bomb as hard as he could. There was a series of dull pops as the CS grenades detonated. Gerber then grabbed the other grenade. He jerked the pin and said, "Now."

All four grenades crashed through the jungle. Gerber hit the ground as did the others. A moment later there were four quick detonations. Dirt rained down and shrapnel slashed through the air. There were a couple of screams and AKs began to fire indiscriminately.

Fetterman was moving immediately to the south, from between the two enemy forces. He hurdled a log, then dived for cover. The rattling of a machine gun cut through the afternoon.

Gerber heard the bolt lock back just before it fired, and he dived. Hoffs yelled a warning that was lost in the burst.

"In front of us," said Fetterman.

Gerber leaped up, ran forward a dozen yards and dived down again. He flipped the selector on his M-16 to a single-shot but didn't have a target.

Fetterman was moving, heading into the thickest part of the vegetation, where the machine gun was hidden. Gerber popped up, fired three quick shots and dived to the right, rolling. The air over him snapped with the sonic crack of the machine-gun bullets. He fired again, one round overhead, trying to keep the machine gunners' attention.

Fetterman was up again, his weapon held at port arms. The selector was on full-auto. He tilted his head, searching for the chattering machine gun.

Then through a gap in the vegetation, he saw the head and helmet of the assistant gunner. A small man in khaki, a pith helmet on his head. Instead of shooting, Fetterman pulled a grenade. He watched as the gunner suddenly appeared, worked the bolt and then dropped out of sight again.

Fetterman slipped carefully to his knee and jerked the pin from the grenade. He aimed the throw, cocked his arm and let fly. As he did, he hit the ground, yelling, "Grenade!"

A moment later there was an explosion, and the machine gun fell silent. Immediately Fetterman was on his feet, moving. He leaped forward to where the twisted wreckage of the machine gun lay. Both the gunner and his assistant were dead, the shrapnel having peppered their sides and back.

Gerber moved forward and dropped to one knee. He saw movement behind Fetterman and fired once. The round took the NVA soldier in the chest, spinning him. He squealed as he tossed his weapon into the air before he collapsed.

"Getting sloppy," said Gerber.

"Knew you were covering."

"Let's get out of here."

"Where're the others?"

Hoffs appeared and said, "Right behind you. McCarthy's watching our rear."

Gerber was going to tell Fetterman to take the point, but there was too much noise now. Shouting in front of them. Screams and orders and then bugles.

"Shit!" said Gerber. "Here they come." He turned to face the threat.

A dozen enemy soldiers appeared, then just as quickly vanished through the gaps in the jungle. Flashes of khaki and faces. Gerber fired at them on single-shot. Fetterman was beside him, blasting away. McCarthy behind them, firing to the rear. Hoffs stood up, fired and then ducked. Rounds were squeezed off as targets appeared. A sporadic rattling of the weapons.

The enemy shot back with AKs. There were two long bursts and then shouts. After a quick volley, someone called in English, "Marine! You die!"

A soldier appeared, head down, bayonet extended. He was growling like a rabid dog, but when Gerber shot him once in the top of the head, he dropped straight down and didn't move.

But there were others. One man shooting from the hip came at them. Gerber fired, missed and fired again. The second round struck him. As dirt flew up from the Vietcong uniform, the enemy gunman squeezed the trigger of his AK, putting a burst into the jungle floor at his own feet.

"Two on the right," yelled Fetterman.

"Reloading here," said Hoffs.

"Clear behind us."

Gerber fired at the two men on the right. One fell into the vegetation, the other dived away and then came up firing. Gerber heard a round snap by his head. With his thumb he flicked the selector to full-auto and fired at the sound. There was a startled scream and then silence.

"Coming up behind us, now," said McCarthy. He opened fire with short bursts.

That was answered by an AK. One weapon on full-auto. The rounds slammed into the trees, stripping the bark.

"Let's go! Let's go," shouted Gerber.

Fetterman moved forward in a crouch, his head swiveling right and left. He found the body of an NVA soldier. The man had lost part of his face and one hand. His still-wet blood had turned the jungle around him slightly crimson. Fetterman picked up his weapon and slung it.

Gerber was next, moving parallel to Fetterman. He stopped near the trunk of a palm, reached out to touch it and went to one knee.

Behind him came a shout. "Grenade!"

Gerber didn't move. He hadn't heard the explosive thrown, and Hoffs was far enough behind him that he was outside the killing zone. He ducked his head and counted to three.

Even as the explosion ripped through the jungle, Hoffs was yelling, "Go! Go!"

Fetterman shouted, "Clear to the front."

Gerber moved toward the master sergeant. He glanced back and saw McCarthy working his way through the jungle. He had lost his boonie hat. He held his weapon up, like a man wading in a chest-high stream.

"Hoffs is behind me."

Gerber whirled and hurried off. He caught Fetterman who had stopped and was staring into the distance.

"There's a couple of guys in front of us still."

"How many?"

"No more than three. Maybe just two."

"Where?"

There was a noise behind them and McCarthy caught up again. Gerber pointed at him and McCarthy turned, facing to the rear, watching.

Fetterman lifted his weapon and sighted. He squeezed the trigger. There was a scream.

"Let's go," he said.

"Hoffs catch us?" Gerber asked.

"Right here," whispered the man, appearing suddenly.

"Let's keep it tight," said Gerber.

Fetterman took off again, running forward. He dodged around a thick stand of trees and bushes, heading back to the west, deeper into Cambodia. They came to a clearing, a huge open meadow. Short grass in the bright afternoon sun.

"To the left," said Gerber.

Fetterman nodded and skirted the meadow, staying inside the trees, hurrying. He leaped a fallen log and then ran forward, where he came to the remains of a bunker. It was old, built years earlier. There was no evidence that the enemy had used it in a long time.

They continued moving. Far behind them came a wild burst of firing. AKs and an RPD. A few Chicom grenades.

Fetterman turned long enough to say, "Sounds like they're shooting up each other." Then he was off again, running back to the east this time, toward South Vietnam.

They kept at it, hurrying on as the sounds of the firing faded. Fetterman led them toward the border, never stopping, never slowing, running forward in a nearly silent half crouch.

After twenty minutes he stopped and dived for cover behind the huge trunk of a tree that was almost four feet in diameter. It would have been the perfect place to make a stand if the enemy attacked and came from the east. If they wanted to make a last stand.

Gerber caught up and dropped to the ground, whipping out his map. As he did, both McCarthy and Hoffs found them. Without a word, McCarthy took a position as a rear guard, and Hoffs slid along the tree trunk as flank security.

"Be a klick to an LZ," said Gerber. "We're in South Vietnam now."

Fetterman moved over and glanced at the map. He studied the ridge lines, the shallow streams and the band of the jungle. ''We head south, be two klicks, but look at all the open ground.''

''We need to get out of here as quickly as possible.''

''Yes, sir.''

Gerber folded the map and stuffed it into his pocket. He glanced at the other two men. Both were drenched with sweat from the run, but neither of them seemed to be breathing hard. They were ready to begin again, as soon as the order was given.

Gerber wiped the sweat off his forehead. He cocked his head, listening, but there were no sounds behind them. If the enemy was chasing them, he was so far behind that he couldn't be heard. Maybe as much as half a klick.

''Let's go, Tony.''

''To the east?''

''To the east.''

Fetterman hesitated a moment. He checked the magazine in his rifle and then moved off to the right, around the tree. This time he kept the pace slower, trying to keep from making noise. He searched the ground around him for booby traps and punji stakes. He listened for sounds that suggested the enemy was near and gaining on him. He found nothing and heard nothing.

It took them nearly thirty minutes to cover the ground to the LZ. They had to avoid a small clearing that might have been large enough for a single chopper, but it would have had to land straight down to avoid the tall trees. In an emergency, maybe, but they had slipped away from the enemy for the moment. It wasn't an emergency.

Fetterman halted them just short of the LZ. He could see it in front of him, the sunlight streaming through gaps in the trees. A bright green glow that marked the end of the quick journey.

As soon as security was out, Gerber took the URC-10, the hand-held UHF radio, and keyed the mike, ''Blackhawk, Blackhawk, this is Zulu. Over.''

There was a long silence and Gerber was about to make the call again when he heard, "Zulu, Zulu, this is Blackhawk Six. Go."

"Roger, Six. We are in need of airlift. One ship."

"Roger, say location."

Gerber tugged the map out and studied it. They hadn't agreed on a code for the coordinates. But he didn't want to give them in the clear.

"Down from Benny's age," began Gerber.

"Roger, Benny's age."

Now Gerber had to add thirty-nine to all of the coordinates so that when they subtracted thirty-nine, he'd have the coordinates of the LZ. A cumbersome system that might not fool the enemy, but certainly better than giving the information in the clear.

Gerber finished the addition and broadcast the numbers. There was silence for a moment and then, "Zulu, this is Blackhawk Six. Inbound your location with the flight. Twenty minutes. Will you throw smoke?"

"Roger, smoke."

Fetterman knelt near Gerber and whispered, "I think we shook them."

"Choppers are inbound. If everything holds the way it is, we'll be out of here in time to have dinner in Saigon."

"You know what that ambush meant, don't you?" said Fetterman.

"Of course."

"So what are you going to do about it?"

"Wait until we get to Saigon and then find the son of a bitch with the big mouth."

"That's what I hoped you'd say."

9

MACV HEADQUARTERS
SAIGON

Jerry Maxwell sat in his office, a file folder in one hand, and looked at Reed who was in the visitor's chair. "How'd the big briefing go?"

"Don't know," said Reed. "The general didn't say a word. He sort of grunted at me, didn't ask a question, and when I was done, he went on to something else."

"Then you did just fine. If you'd fucked it up, you'd have heard about it before you left the room. He'd have whispered a comment to a colonel who'd have found you."

"Then I must've done all right."

Maxwell turned his attention back to the file.

"You know any more about the leak?" asked Reed, smiling.

Maxwell closed the folder and looked at the younger man. "This is no laughing matter. We fuck up in here, let information out, and men die."

"I didn't mean to imply that I didn't take it seriously," he said.

Maxwell turned so that he could stare at Reed. "Let me tell you something. In espionage, we find a double agent, someone working for us who is also working for the enemy, the man has a fatal accident."

Reed couldn't help himself. He laughed at that. "You've been watching too many James Bond movies."

"Don't fool yourself about that," said Maxwell. "And if you don't think we'd do it, remember, there's the Special Forces involved. They'd shoot a traitor as fast as they would a Vietcong attacking the wire. Those are the men with their lives on the line. They'll kill the traitor first chance they get. They won't hesitate."

"Come on," said Reed. "I've read about all those old spies in prison being traded for one another."

"Sure," said Maxwell, "if they have one of ours and we think it's important to keep the double alive. If not, he dies. You don't hear about that."

Reed nodded solemnly and wondered why Maxwell had suddenly felt the urge to share that with him. Was it some kind of veiled warning, or was it just because he had made that crack about the James Bond movies? Maxwell might be trying to convince him how serious the business was. It might easily be nothing more than that.

But even as he rationalized the warning, he felt his stomach turn to ice. Fear burned through him and his heart hammered. He tried to keep his face calm, sure that Maxwell didn't mean anything, but afraid that he did.

As calmly as he could, he said, "If we had a leak, if someone talked about that patrol, it had to be one of the Cambodians."

Maxwell nodded. "That would be the first thing you'd think."

"But you say that as if you don't believe it."

"The Cambodes hate the Vietnamese. I can't see them helping the Communists."

"But will they help the South Vietnamese?" asked Reed, thinking he'd found a flaw.

"Except that to help the South Vietnamese would keep the North Vietnamese out of Cambodia. A victory in the South would ensure that they don't have to fight the Vietnamese."

"Sophisticated thinking," said Reed.

"Which seems to be the flaw in my theory," said Maxwell. "I'm not sure that the peasant in the field is sophisticated enough to come up with that. So, you're right. The Cambodians are the most likely candidates. But we won't know until Gerber and Fetterman return."

"I take it," said Reed, "that there are still no reports from the patrol."

"That went without saying."

Reed felt that the danger had passed. He sat up straighter and asked, "So what's next?"

"I've got some work to do while I wait to hear from Gerber and Fetterman."

"How do you know they'll be back?" asked Reed. "Maybe they'll walk into an ambush."

"Fetterman would never walk into an ambush, unless he had a reason to do so."

"No one's that good," said Reed.

"Fetterman is."

Reed clapped his hands. "If you've nothing for me, I think I'll run along for a while."

"Go ahead," said Maxwell. "Just stay close in case I need some help."

Reed got up and walked to the door, pausing to look back at Maxwell who was now hunched over his desk, reading a file. Reed closed the door quietly as he left.

THE PICKUP WENT OFF without a hitch. When Gerber spotted the flight, far to the south, he tossed a green smoke grenade into the center of the LZ. As the helicopters got closer, the four men moved out where they could be seen by the flight leader. The trail ship broke off, and under cover of the gunships, landed in the middle of the LZ. Almost before the skids were on the ground, Gerber and the men were swarming on board; and before they were in the cargo compartment, the aircraft was up, flying toward the trees. The gunships hovered around, looking for the enemy, but the VC and NVA had been left behind in the jungle.

Gerber scrambled into the cargo compartment and then knelt between the seats of the pilots. Over the screaming turbines he yelled, "Can you take us to Saigon?"

"Wait one," responded the pilot.

Gerber saw the pilot's lips moving as he talked on the radio. Finally he turned and held a thumb up. "We'll take you to Hotel Three."

"Land us at MACV?" asked Gerber.

"No problem."

With that, Gerber moved back to the troop seat and sat down. He put on the seat belt, locking himself in and then leaned back against the soft gray soundproofing of the transmission wall. He glanced at Fetterman and then the other two men. All were dirty, sweat-soaked and tired-looking. They hadn't been in the field that long, but the heat, the humidity and the strain sapped strength quickly. Once the pressure was off and the men could relax, it seemed that they were all on the verge of exhaustion.

Gerber felt it himself. The air at altitude, though not very cold, was blowing into the cargo compartment. As his clothes dried, he felt a chill. He closed his eyes for a moment, letting the feeling take over. He felt the ache in his bones, felt the strain of his muscles. A run through the jungle under any circumstances was a difficult task, but when the enemy was close, it became an almost impossible thing. Run and don't stop, as the heat tried to kill you. Run, even though your mouth was filled with cotton and the pain radiated from your chest, up into your shoulders and arms and threatened to kill you. Run, because the enemy was behind you and wanted to kill you. No time to think. Just time to run.

He wiped his face with the sleeve of his uniform. He pulled the magazine out of the weapon. Then he ejected the live round and picked it up.

"What are we going to do in Saigon, Captain?" asked Fetterman, yelling over the noise of the chopper.

"Go see Maxwell and tell him what we know."

"And then?"

Gerber looked at Fetterman, wondering what he wanted to know. There was more to the question than wondering what they would do in Saigon. But it wasn't time to discuss it. They'd have to relate what they knew to Maxwell and then see what happened there.

Gerber looked out the cargo compartment door. Below him were the rice paddies of the farmers, a cluster of thatched hootches, and a man walking behind a water buffalo. The rice paddies gave way to a light forest and the rubber plantations to the north of Highway One, along the Song Sai Gon. They followed the river for a while, staying north of Cu Chi. They then flew to the north of Saigon to where the river seemed to spread out and the greens of the vegetation gave way to the light browns and reds of the earth.

The crew chief leaned around from the well and shouted, "We're about five out."

"Thanks," yelled Gerber.

"What do we do on the ground, sir?" asked McCarthy.

"Stay out of trouble. We'll debrief with Maxwell and then get transport over to Tan Son Nhut."

"You going to need us again?" asked Hoffs.

"I wouldn't think so. Have a night on the town. If anything develops, I'll let you know."

Hoffs looked at Gerber as if he hadn't quite understood the last of that. The noise from the helicopter, the screaming of the turbine and the popping of the blades, seemed to have gotten louder. Sound reverberated through the interior of the chopper, making it nearly impossible to hear.

When they turned, and began to descend, Gerber picked out the MACV building, a low affair that seemed to sit on top of a slight hill, much like the temples erected in Central America that dominated the surrounding countryside. MACV was on the highest ground with a parking lot of crushed gravel to one side. Guardhouses and sandbag walls were ranged near the street. A helipad sat on the expanse of lawn in front of the building. There wasn't much around it to suggest that a war was going on.

They shot an approach to the center of the pad, a rubberized area of dirty black held down by sandbags. There were lights on each of the four corners, and a tall fence between the pad and the MACV building, which looked like a backstop on a baseball diamond.

As they settled in, the rotors kicked up a cloud of red dust that swirled around them, obscuring their view. Loose paper, trash, grass and debris were swept up and thrown around, some of it snagging in the backstop and hanging there, unable to get past it.

Once they touched down, Gerber leaped out and hurried to the side of the pad. He crouched there with his back to the chopper. When the others joined him, the cloud of dust got thicker and the helicopter came to a hover. It turned and then lifted off, climbing out toward the north and the Saigon River. When it was gone, there was little sound. Traffic on the street, a horn and some music, but in comparison it seemed to be quiet.

After the helicopter disappeared, Gerber began to walk toward the double doors. Fetterman caught up with him. "We're not going to be real popular in there."

"Why? Because we just came from the field?"

"Uh-huh. The Saigon commandos don't like to be reminded that there are some of us who get out into the field once in a while."

"Well, that's just tough."

"Yes, sir."

Hoffs moved in front of them and opened the first of the doors. As he stood there, the air-conditioning from the interior leaked into the area between the doors and he said, "I could get used to this."

"Used to what?" asked Gerber.

"Air-conditioning."

"Well, I wouldn't," said McCarthy. "The brass might be living in comfort, but that's never going to filter down to the rest of us. We don't have the juice."

Gerber entered, moved into the building and then toward the steps that led down. He stopped there and pointed down one of the long, almost deserted hallways. "There's a dayroom about halfway down there. Has a TV, magazines and it used to have a refrigerator with soft drinks in it. Why don't you two wait in there? If we need you, we'll call for you."

McCarthy grinned. "You're not going to hurt my feelings by sending me away to sit around and drink cold Coke. I'll see you down there."

Gerber and Fetterman descended into the basement, signed in at the iron gate and then walked toward Maxwell's office. Gerber knocked and then turned the knob, finding the door unlocked. He opened it and stepped in.

"Back already?" asked Maxwell. He stopped and looked at their faces. "Not good, is it?"

"If we're back, Jerry, it's not good," said Gerber. "We found them. Dead. Ambushed."

"Shit. I knew it."

"Yes, you did," said Fetterman. "Why?"

"Sit down and we'll talk," said Maxwell.

KINSON WOKE UP SLOWLY, feeling slightly sick to his stomach. His body was hot, uncomfortable, and his arms and legs hurt. He didn't move though, listening to the sounds of the jungle around him. There didn't seem to be anything there, other than the insects, animals and birds that belonged there. No people anywhere.

Slowly he rolled away from the spiny trunk of the bush onto his back and looked up at the canopy. Through the gaps he could see bright blue sky. It was late in the afternoon, but it was still daylight.

Kinson sat up gingerly, pulled out his canteen and drank the rest of the water. The water had a plastic taste to it and was hot, but wet enough to quench his thirst. That left one full canteen for the night and the next day.

His stomach cramped slightly. He wanted to eat. He was hungry, but he didn't want to make the effort. Instead he stood up, tightened the sling of his rifle and moved toward the trunk of one of the tall trees. He used it as a latrine and felt better. Rubbing his face, he decided that he wasn't going to wait until dark. It was time to get moving. With some luck he could be picked up yet that day.

He checked his rifle, made sure that he hadn't shoved the barrel into the dirt while he slept, and then moved to the edge of the bush-choked thicket. It was a mistake to let impatience force him out, but he couldn't help it. He had to get going. If he moved slowly, carefully, he should be fine. The enemy would be pulling in the day units, and it would be a couple of hours before the night patrols and ambushes were dispatched.

He came to the edge of the undergrowth. Now he could see farther into the jungle, about ten yards. All around him were small trees, bushes, ferns and vines. Nothing like the area in which he had hidden, where the vegetation was so thick he hadn't been able to see more than a foot or so.

As he moved out into the jungle, it suddenly seemed a bit cooler, a couple of degrees at the most. He wiped the sweat from his face again and began to walk toward the east. He moved slowly, deliberately, watching and listening.

The jungle was quiet. He stopped once, stared through a gap in the wall of vegetation where he thought he saw a man waiting. An enemy soldier. But the man didn't move and Kinson realized that he was looking at a combination of shadows and plants. It was just his imagination.

He started off again, sliding around the trees and between the bushes. He moved with care, using his feet to feel his way along, listening for sounds that the enemy was near, watching, his senses alert. No one would be able to sneak up on him.

He stopped frequently to listen, but there was never anything to hear. He checked his map, but that didn't provide much help. There were no landmarks. Except a stream, about half a klick in front of him. If he found it, it wouldn't mean much. Streams in the jungle changed course with the seasons. A heavy rain could easily alter its path. What he needed was to get out of the jungle and into some open country. Country where there were some roads, villages, streams, hills, ridges, anything other than the endless monotony of the jungle.

Finally, overhead, he heard the sounds of a helicopter. One, maybe two of them, flying high. It wasn't important that the canopy concealed him and made it impossible for the crews to see him. What was important was that they were overhead. It meant that he had made it back into South Vietnam. Now there was a chance that he would be rescued.

He stopped to study the map. All around him was jungle. In some directions it stretched for miles and would take days to get through. In others, he could pop out in a klick or two. South, southeast seemed to be the direction he needed to go. He would move into an area of rice paddies and swamps. Open ground where a helicopter could spot him.

He folded the map and put it away. He opened his last canteen and took a deep drink. Then, feeling renewed, he started off. Still he was careful, but he picked up the pace. He wanted to get to the open and get the hell out of the jungle.

Just as he had begun to believe that he had misread his map, he saw a glow in front of him. It penetrated the jungle and told him that the canopy was gone. He hurried toward it until he could see the edge of the trees. Then he slowed, working his way to the very edge where he could look out into the open rice paddies.

"I made it," he told himself. "I made it." And then realized that he hadn't yet. His chances had improved greatly. He was out of Cambodia and he was near open ground where American patrols or helicopters could find him. All he had to do was be patient.

For a few moments he crouched at the edge of the jungle, watching as an old woman walked from a mud hootch. She stooped, picked up something and then returned to the hootch. A man in black shorts appeared, turned and then ran, heading for a clump of trees not far from the mud hootch. And then a group of men appeared. First one, then another and another. It looked as if a platoon was filtering out of the trees on the far side of the hootch.

Before they had moved far, the old woman ran from her protection and a man shouted at her. She stopped and turned, walking back to them. Kinson wondered what was going on, and then realized he was watching an American sweep-and-destroy mission. Americans.

"Yeah!" he said, almost shouting. He stood up, waiting a moment and then stepped from the trees. It was all he could do to keep from running toward them. He needed to walk slowly, his weapon held out so they could see it was an M-16. Walk slowly so they'd know he wasn't a threat. His size and uniform would identify him as an American. There shouldn't be a problem.

He was halfway across the rice paddy when one of the soldiers turned toward him, raising his rifle. Kinson stopped immediately and lifted his M-16 high over his head.

"Hey!" he yelled. "American soldier."

Two men turned toward him. One of them said something to the other and they began to walk in his direction. Kinson didn't move. He didn't have to.

When the others got close, the taller, older of the two asked, "Who are you?"

"Staff Sergeant Perry Kinson. My men and I walked into an ambush last night. I'm the only survivor."

"What the hell are you doing out here?"

"Christ, sir, give the guy a break," said the other. "Come on in. We'll have the medic take a look at you."

Kinson grinned, the excitement flooding through him. He wanted to scream and shout, to leap around like a kid, but didn't. Instead he said, "I've got to get back to MACV and make my report."

The officer said, "We've got choppers on standby. We can probably scare up a ride."

"Thank you . . ."

"Dickson, Lieutenant Dickson, First Infantry Division."

"Yes, sir. The Big Red One. Anything you can do would be greatly appreciated."

"Come on," said the other man. "Medic will look at you and then we'll get you something to drink while you wait for the chopper."

"Sounds great!" said Kinson. He knew that his words were inadequate to express what he was suddenly feeling, but he didn't know what else to say. The rest of his men were dead in the jungle, and it was the first time since the battle that he had thought of them.

"We'll get even," he promised them.

Dickson stopped and asked, "What was that?"

"Nothing," said Kinson. "Nothing."

10

Gerber sat in the visitor's chair. He had unbuckled his pistol belt and stripped off his rucksack, dropping it to the floor. He had set his weapon in the corner out of the way. He didn't bother to check his pistol, concealed under his jungle jacket, knowing a round was chambered so that it was ready to fire.

Fetterman did the same and then took his position by the file cabinets. He leaned on the top of one, studying the file folders scattered across the top without any real interest of what was in them.

"Okay, Jerry, now we can talk." Gerber stared at the CIA man. He didn't think that Maxwell was the leak, but at the moment, everything pointed at him. Maxwell had said that no one was going to know the patrol was going out, and yet they had been ambushed. It meant that Maxwell had told someone something that he shouldn't have. Gerber was going to withhold judgment until he had all the facts.

Maxwell turned to give Gerber his full attention. "Okay, you say my boys were ambushed. Anything unusual about that?"

"Hard to say. We didn't have much time on the site. I wouldn't expect an ambush patrol out in Cambodia. That in and of itself makes it unusual."

"Why didn't you have time?"

Fetterman answered that. "We got ambushed, too. Someone walked up on us while we were there." Fetterman's voice was tight. He too was angry.

Maxwell shot him a glance and wondered what was going on. He didn't mention that. Instead he said, "But that shouldn't be strange. Enemy returning to pick up equipment."

"No, Jerry," said Gerber, "you miss the point. The bodies had been pretty well stripped. The enemy had gotten everything that he wanted. Even cut open the pockets to steal the wallets. Nothing left for him to get."

"That would mean . . ."

"Exactly," snapped Gerber. "You've got a fat leak here. One with a direct pipeline into the enemy camp. A leak right out of this office."

"Now wait a minute," said Maxwell. "You can't possibly think that I'm the one—"

"All I know," interrupted Gerber, his voice taking on a hard edge, "is that you said you weren't letting anyone know that we were going out into the field, but once we're there, the enemy knew we were out."

Maxwell held up a hand and nodded quickly. "Now wait a minute here. Just wait a minute." He stared at the top of his desk. "I know I said no one else would know, but I couldn't keep that promise. Pittman in the radio room knew, as did a couple of the watch officers, and I did coordinate with the liaison office upstairs. I didn't want someone clearing an Arclight because they didn't know we had troops in there."

"Jesus Christ in a B-52," said Gerber. He leaned back in the chair suddenly, swiping at the sweat on his forehead. "Don't fucking tell me that you're keeping anything a secret if you're not planning on doing it. Those the only people who knew?''

"Reed knows, too. Saw you leaving the office and figured I had told you to head out into the field."

From the corner Fetterman said, "No surprise that this place is full of leaks. You're not going to tell anyone, and suddenly half the people around here have to know."

"Reed thinks it was the Cambodians."

"He would," said Gerber.

"No," said Fetterman. "Absolutely no way."

"Why not?"

Gerber took over again. He rubbed a hand across his mouth and chin. "Cambodes didn't know we were going in. That lets them out right now."

"But not for last night," said Maxwell.

"Jerry, they're both dead," said Fetterman. "Why are they dead if they worked for the enemy?"

"Maybe because they were burned as sources. Charlie knew they'd be the first people we'd suspect, so he killed them to protect their other sources in the same place. They don't care about the Cambodians."

"Won't wash," said Gerber. "They were enemies of the VC. Hell, the enemy mutilated the bodies. That means neither one were our sources."

"They still could have been the ones who talked."

"Jerry, you're not listening," said Fetterman. He turned and faced Maxwell. "Maybe they were the sources, maybe they got killed by accident. Hell, it's dark in the jungle. They might have been caught in the cross fire. But even with that the VC wouldn't mutilate the bodies. That would be an act that was counterproductive."

"I don't understand," said Maxwell.

"Christ, you're supposed to be the fucking intelligence agent around here," said Gerber, "and you don't understand the local customs. If the Cambodes learn that the Vietnamese multilate the bodies of their allies they won't get any more help. The Cambodes will withstand torture to remain loyal, but you mess up the body and you condemn the spirit to walking the earth eternally. No reward in heaven or whatever.''

"I still don't see . . .''

"Jerry, the Cambodians will put up with a lot of shit, but don't mess with the dead. The VC were sending the Cambodes a message. Don't work for the Americans or you'll be doomed for all eternity. The Cambodes are not the leak,'' said Fetterman.

"Okay, they're eliminated,'' said Maxwell.

Gerber turned and stared at the intelligence agent. "So now we're right back to you and the MACV empire.''

"I suppose so.''

"The leak has to be right here under your nose, and it would seem that we should be able to figure it out. Who all did you tell?''

"I told you. And then they could have told others.''

"Shit,'' said Fetterman. "Throw a rock into the pool.''

"What does that mean?'' asked Maxwell.

Gerber was getting impatient. "It means, Jerry, that the circle of knowledge expands outward until it sounds like everyone who walked into the building was briefed on our activities.''

"It's not that bad.''

"No,'' said Fetterman. "It just seems that everyone knew. No one put out a memo or erected a billboard.''

There was a knock on the door. Maxwell looked up and then yelled, "Come.''

The MP opened the door and stepped in. He held two Cokes in his hand. "Sergeant up there said to deliver these to Captain Gerber and Sergeant Fetterman.''

Fetterman moved to the door and took the cold cans. "Thank you.''

The MP nodded and closed the door.

"Shit, you could have ordered me one," said Maxwell.

Fetterman handed a can to Gerber and said, "We didn't order these. One of our boys, Hoffs or McCarthy, was thinking of us. Not a situation you find in MACV. People taking care of one another." He pulled the pop top, dropped the tab into the can and then drank. "Yeah. He was thinking of us."

Gerber opened his, drank and then said, "What's your next move, Jerry?"

Maxwell opened his drawer and pulled out a yellow legal pad. He flipped over the top sheet. "Trouble seems to have started after Tet. Oh, we always had trouble when dealing with the South Vietnamese, but this is something new. I've written down the names of everyone who was assigned to us since Tet. Both military and civilian."

"So now we have to design a mission for each name," Gerber said with a nod of his head. "Pass the information to each of the men and see which one gets leaked to the enemy. That's providing you can keep the details secret from everyone except the man who's supposed to get it."

"Look," said Maxwell, his voice rising. "I'm not incompetent. I know my job."

"Could have fooled me," Fetterman muttered.

"That's uncalled for," shouted Maxwell.

"No, Jerry," said Gerber quietly. "It's not uncalled for. Not when the enemy knows we're in the field. Now, you have any clue about who the leak might be?"

"Only based on the fact that we didn't have a problem until these new men were assigned."

"I don't like to think that it's an American," said Fetterman, shaking his head.

Maxwell looked at him. "I think that might be why this has gone on as long as it has. No one wants to think an American would go over to the enemy."

There was another knock on the door. Maxwell rolled his eyes toward the ceiling. "It's becoming busier than Tan Son Nhut." He raised his voice. "Come."

Reed opened the door and said, "Oh, I didn't know that you were busy."

Maxwell waved him in, glad to have someone else in the room with him. Someone who could divert some of the anger from him. "No. Come on in. Captain Gerber says that the Cambodes couldn't have been the leak."

Reed looked at the Special Forces officer. "You're sure, sir?"

"Positive. They were killed in the ambush."

"That doesn't mean . . ."

"Forget it," said Maxwell. "They weren't the leak."

Reed nodded. He glanced at Gerber and then back at Fetterman. "I just stopped by to see if there was anything else that you needed."

Maxwell hesitated and then said, "Not today. Head on home."

"Thanks," said Reed. He headed to the door without a word to either of the Special Forces men.

"Hold it," ordered Fetterman. "You knew we were going into the field."

Reed stopped and stared at the master sergeant. He wasn't sure how to respond. Finally he said, "Yes, I suppose so."

"Where have you been?"

"I'm not sure I have to answer that." He glanced at Maxwell.

"Go ahead," said Maxwell.

Reed nodded and said, "I've been here."

"More to the point," said Fetterman. "You tell anyone about our mission?"

"Hey, I'm not stupid."

"Answer the question," said Fetterman.

"No, I didn't tell anyone. I know enough to keep my mouth shut."

"Not out and about, telling the girls how important you are? Not out there shooting your mouth off to prove that you're on the inside here?"

"I resent the question."

"Fine," said Fetterman. "Resent it. But it wasn't your ass getting shot at."

Reed stared at Fetterman and finally dropped his eyes. "I didn't tell anyone," he said.

Maxwell broke in, "Why don't you get out of here?"

Reed nodded and left. As soon as the door was closed, Gerber turned to Maxwell. "He on your list?"

"Yes, but I doubt he's the leak. He had a good background check and clearance when he arrived here. His pedigree is among the best."

"I don't like him," said Gerber.

"Why?"

Gerber shrugged. "I can't put a finger on it."

"It was because he was so ready to blame the Cambodes," said Fetterman. "Even after you told him they were not the leak, he tried to push them as the answer."

"He's at the bottom of the list," said Maxwell.

"Not mine," said Gerber.

"A personal dislike is no reason to assume that he's the bad guy."

"It'll do until I can think of a better one. He tops my list."

Maxwell turned so that he could lean his elbows on his desk. The legal pad was centered between his arms. "I'll go over the list, and then we'll design a strategy."

"Go ahead," said Gerber. "I'm all ears."

REED GOT OUT OF THERE as quickly as he could. He didn't know why the two Special Forces men didn't believe the Cambodes were the leak, but they were sure. He'd thought that dead men could tell no tales, but these two dead Cambodians seemed to shout answers.

Not that it mattered. With the Cambodes out as the source, Reed knew who the next victim could be, and he knew that attention had to be diverted to someone else quickly. The questioning in Maxwell's office proved that. Now that he needed to think of another scapegoat, there was one name that came immediately to mind.

Pittman.

The man had no class. He was a gross, obnoxious loudmouth who couldn't be trusted. Reed smiled. He'd have to find a way to let Maxwell know that Pittman was the leak. That would take some thinking. Something he'd have to figure out by morning.

But that would be in the morning. Now he'd just get out, drive over to see Thi. His smile widened as he thought about her. He felt his heart begin to beat faster but realized that it was lust. That's all it had ever been. He couldn't really love a Vietnamese woman. They just didn't have the sophistication to stay up with an American man.

He left the MACV Headquarters, walked to his jeep and unlocked the wheel. He climbed in, started it and decided that he had to see Thi. Had to talk to her again. Maybe his inspiration would come from her.

As he drove through the streets of Saigon, looking over his shoulder frequently, he was afraid that he was being followed. Then, suddenly, he realized that his jeep had white numbers stenciled on the front and rear bumpers. Anyone with half a brain would know whose jeep it was. The numbers would lead investigators right back to him. He couldn't drive it over to Thi's.

He turned around and drove into the downtown area. He parked the jeep, locked up the steering wheel and then walked away. He turned a corner and found the streets alive with people. GIs in khaki uniforms or civilian clothes, Vietnamese men wearing Western-style clothes and Vietnamese women in short skirts and tight blouses. Noise from bars, music, shouting, arguments, filtered onto the streets. There were car horns and the rumble of truck engines. The streets were almost filled, from the buildings on one side to the walls on the other.

He moved to the curb, waited and saw an empty taxi. As he raised a hand to call to it, the driver spotted him. It dived out of traffic and squealed to a halt inches from him. Reed opened the back door and crawled in.

''Where you go, Joe?''

Reed leaned forward, his arms resting on the seat in front of him. He told the driver where he wanted to go. The man glanced up at the mirror and then grinned.

''Sure, Joe.''

As Reed sat back, the driver rocketed into traffic, causing horns to blare and tires to squeal. He whipped around a corner, barely slowing, then shot around two Army trucks. The soldiers shouted and flipped him the finger. Reed wasn't happy with the attention the driver was drawing to himself, but then people would remember the crazy driver and cab, not the American riding in the rear.

They came to a cross street and the taxi slowed. The scenery had changed from the stately buildings erected by the French, the stores built by the Americans and the structures of the rich Vietnamese, to the low houses of the poor. Concrete tubes that had been designed for sewers were being used as houses. Families lived in cardboard packing crates and wooden crates. A hundred people, a thousand, milled around with nothing to do. The air was heavy with the stench of humanity. Unwashed bodies, open sewers and stagnant water.

They turned again, this time onto a residential street. Reed had him stop the taxi a few houses away and paid the first price the driver named. He scrambled from the back seat and stood there as the driver took off, throwing up a rooster tail of dust and gravel.

As the taxi disappeared around the corner, the kids descended on him, hands up, demanding cigarettes, money and candy. He pushed through the crowd, ignoring them. When they saw he had nothing for them, they vanished as quickly as they had appeared.

Reed walked up to the door and knocked on it. He stood to one side, like a police officer searching for a crook. When Thi opened up, he leaped forward, grinning.

Thi was surprised. She let out a shriek and jumped back. But then she recognized him and began to giggle. "You frightened me," she said.

"Good," said Reed. "Everyone should be frightened once in a while."

She threw herself at him then, hugging him. "You surprised me too. I did not expect to see you so early."

"Things change," said Reed. He separated himself from her and walked into the living room. He sat down and watched as she stood in the doorway, staring at him.

Reed raised a hand and she moved toward him. She stopped near his side and he ran his hand up the back of her thigh, up under her short skirt. He touched her silk panties and slipped his hand around her leg so that his thumb could press against her.

"You are in a hurry today," she said.

"No," said Reed. "Not in a hurry." But he didn't move his hand. He slipped his thumb under the light fabric to touch her gently. She pressed forward slightly and he could tell that she was ready.

Reed pulled her closer and then reached up with his free hand, dragging her panties lower. She moaned quietly and said, "We could go upstairs."

"No," said Reed. "Not yet. Not quite yet." He used his hand and fingers, feeling the sparse pubic hair.

Her knees buckled slightly, forcing her body down on his hand. She groaned with pleasure. Her hips moved gently, no more than a couple of inches in any direction as she tried to help him.

"So close," she said suddenly.

He pulled his hand away from her. Her eyes snapped open then and she looked down at him. "Why?"

"To make it last. To draw it out." He rubbed her thigh and cupped her bottom as she stood there trembling. He reached up to unbutton her blouse. She shrugged it away, leaving herself naked to the hips.

"Let's go upstairs," she said, her voice husky. "Please, let's go."

Reed stood up and kissed her, first on the lips and then the chin, working his way lower until he took her left breast in his mouth. He bit the nipple gently, feeling it grow hard as she moaned again and again.

He unfastened her skirt and pushed it over her hips so that it fell to the floor. Standing there naked, her panties around her ankles, she pressed herself against him as his hands explored her body.

"Now it's time to go upstairs," he said.

"Oh, yes," she said.

"You go on up. I will be there in a moment. I need to lock the door so we won't be interrupted."

Without a word she turned and fled. She ran up the stairs as Reed stood below and watched the flexing of the muscles in her legs and back. It was a pretty picture. One that he wished he could preserve, but he hadn't thought of that. He should have brought a camera.

As she disappeared up there, Reed turned and locked the door. He then walked into the kitchen, found a set of knives and selected one. The blade wasn't more than six inches long, but there was a point and it was sharp. It would do.

He slipped it into the back pocket of his pants and then headed upstairs. He found Thi lying on her bed, her hands behind her head, her body displayed for him, a light coating of sweat making it shine. As he entered the room, she rolled to her side and lifted one leg slightly.

''Hello,'' she said.

Watching her, Reed took off his clothes, setting them down carefully on a chair well away from the bed. He then moved to her, gently pushed her back and sat down next to her. He kissed her mouth and chin, beginning to explore her torso. She was silent, taking it, trying not to move. As his hands and tongue probed lower, she couldn't help herself. She shuddered, groaned and said, ''Please don't stop.''

He lifted his feet and stretched out next to her, finally rolling toward her until they were joined. He moved slowly and she responded, at first as slowly, but then trying to pick up the pace, slamming her hips against his body.

Both of them lost control then. They twisted around into a better position. Reed matched her speed and felt it building inside him from a hidden center. He forced the feeling down, holding it off until she screamed her pleasure. Then, knowing what would happen in a few minutes, he gave up his control, whipping his hips against her as he clutched her to him, biting at her shoulder.

They collapsed together, neither of them having the strength to move. Neither of them wanting to move. Their sweat mingled but didn't dry in the humidity of Saigon.

Finally Reed rolled to his right. He felt her shift and lift a leg, bringing it up so that her knee was against his belly.

''That was the best,'' she said. ''The very best.''

''Yeah.''

They were quiet for a moment and then she moved again, sitting up. ''We could shower and then go out to find something to eat.''

''All right,'' said Reed, but he didn't move right away. He turned so that he could look at her. ''You're so beautiful.''

''That's the first time you ever said anything like that to me.''

"It's true," he said.

"There is something different about you today," she said, reaching out to stroke him. "Less fire. Less hate. You are almost calm."

"It's being with you."

She pulled away and stood up, moving toward the wardrobe. She took out a short silk robe and started to put it on.

"You don't need that," said Reed.

She tossed it to the side and walked slowly to the door, letting him look at her. She glanced over her shoulder at him. "You coming?" She headed off to the bathroom.

Reed moved to his clothes and took the knife from his pocket. He followed her down the hall and caught up with her in the bathroom. As he entered, she turned and he stepped close as if to kiss her. She tilted her head and closed her eyes, waiting for him.

At that moment he struck. He brought the knife up sharply from behind his back and drove it into her stomach. She gasped in surprise and pain, staggering away from him. For a moment she was too stunned to realize what had happened. Her hands were on her belly as blood began to flow rapidly.

She stared at her bloodstained hands and then up into Reed's eyes. She didn't speak to him. It was as if he had handed her a snake. It was so totally unexpected that she didn't know how to react to it.

Reed was surprised too. He had thought that she would fall down dead. That's what happened in the movies and on television. Stab someone and that was it. A body on the floor. He moved in, thrust again and heard the blade scrape on the bone of her ribs.

Suddenly she screamed. She lifted her hands to push him away and then balled them into fists. She swung at him, still screaming. She tried to fight him off with the weak blows of her fists. Now he was frightened that someone would hear her. He stabbed again and again. Jerking the knife out and plunging it into her body in a frenzy. Blood spattered and spurted. It splashed against the walls and floor.

Thi fell to the rear, against the wall. Now her hands were at her sides. She was too weak to raise them. She glanced at her body, a crimson mess, leaking blood. She collapsed to the floor and turned her face to him, but didn't have the energy to ask him, "Why?"

Reed backed away from her. He crouched in the doorway, staring at her body, watching the blood pool around her. He wanted to touch her, tell her that he was sorry, but his mouth was dry and his throat constricted. With a shaking hand he reached for a towel and wiped the handle of the knife, dropping it to the floor.

It was then that he thought of fingerprints. There was no way he could retrace his steps and wipe away all his fingerprints. Not after weeks of seeing her. It would be an impossible task.

He stood up and looked into the blood-spattered mirror. So much blood covered his body, too, that it looked as if he had been injured in a fight. He turned, looked at the shower and then stepped into it. Using his palm, he turned it on, adjusted the water and calmly washed off every trace of Thi's blood, using the perfumed soap that she had been so proud of.

He turned off the water, dried himself, and carefully left the bathroom. He didn't want to step in the blood. And now, he couldn't look at Thi's body. He could pretend that it wasn't there, that she was alive somewhere else in the house, but he couldn't look at her.

In the bedroom he dressed quickly and then moved to the window. At first he had planned to get out as soon as the deed was done, but now he decided to wait until dark. Wait until it was hard to see a single person walking in the gloom. Wait until all the adults were off the street in the neighborhood, hiding behind their closed doors. Then it would be time to get out of Thi's house, but not before.

He sat down in a chair away from the window and watched the sun as it set, pretending that he was waiting for Thi to return. He was angry with her for standing him up, but he'd get over it. She'd apologize, she'd strip her clothes, and all would be forgotten.

That's what he told himself. That was what he believed.

11

CARASEL HOTEL

Gerber paced around his room, touching things but not settling down. Fetterman sat in the chair. Morrow reclined on the bed, a drink in her hand. They had left MACV, come to the hotel to shower and change, and then met in Gerber's room. Maxwell had reluctantly agreed to keep their rucksacks and other gear locked in his office. Morrow had shown up unannounced, five minutes earlier. She had only wanted a drink, so Gerber had given her some Beam's with a splash of water.

Gerber finally turned and looked at the master sergeant.

"It's not going to change anything, Captain."

Morrow watched, sipping her drink and didn't ask a question. She had learned long ago that sometimes it was best to pretend that you just didn't exist. That way people would sometimes forget you were there and say things they'd prefer you didn't hear.

Gerber rubbed his face. "It's really Maxwell's job. He's the one who's familiar with the terrain."

"I would agree, sir, except he'd have folded his tent with the belief that the Cambodes set the thing up and then were so stupid they walked into it too."

"But I don't see a way to get a handle on it. There's no place for us to go."

Fetterman shrugged. "Look, we know that the problem evolved after . . ." He stopped and looked at Morrow.

"Don't mind me," she said. "I won't tell anyone."

Gerber glanced at her and then said, "We've already said so much, a little more won't matter. Besides, if I didn't trust her, I wouldn't have said a word in the first place."

Morrow took another drink. "I take it you're worried about the leak in MACV."

"Yes," said Fetterman slowly, as if surprised that she knew about it.

"Hell, Tony, everyone knows that the place is full of leaks. We've all got our pet sources over there." She grinned and added, "Mine's Maxwell, as if you didn't know."

Gerber nodded toward her. "Maybe she can help."

"Tell me what I need to know."

Fetterman stood up and walked around to the back of the chair. He leaned on it, staring down at her. "Someone is passing information to the enemy. We suspect that it's one of the new people assigned there. The problem is, if we factor in the military types, which seems very unlikely now, then we've nearly two hundred names on the list."

"But without them, just the civilians, then we've got twelve people to worry about," said Gerber.

"Why not simply eliminate the soldiers?" said Morrow.

"Because that—" Gerber stopped. "You know, a word in the right place and we could get them all assigned somewhere else. The problem surfaces in their new location, and we've got our man. Christ, that's simple."

"So then," continued Fetterman, "we're stuck with the new civilians, and you don't like that Reed . . ."

"Maxwell's assistant?" asked Morrow.

"That what he is?" Gerber's voice was tinged with sarcasm.

Morrow shrugged and held up her drink for a refill. Gerber got the bottle out of the wardrobe and darkened her drink. And then asked again, "That what he is?"

"Well," said Morrow, "that's what everyone tells me. Maxwell didn't want him, but he was told he'd been assigned to him. Showed up at his door assigned to him."

"If anyone listened to what the South Vietnamese said, I'd believe he's our man. But who the hell listens to the Vietnamese."

"Captain, that didn't make sense."

"It meant simply that the Vietnamese wouldn't be able to force someone on us."

Morrow stood up and walked around the end of the bed and sat down again. "So what are you going to do?"

"I don't think that's up to us," said Gerber.

"Except," Fetterman offered, "Maxwell came to us because he trusts us. We've got to do something."

Gerber shrugged. "I only have one idea."

"What's that?"

"Get something to eat."

THE LAST OF THE SUNLIGHT faded, and there were no streetlights to illuminate the area. Reed stood up, careful not to touch anything. He returned to the bathroom, and again avoided looking at the body. Instead he crouched and picked up the knife. He examined it like an archeologist studying a stone tool. There were flecks of blood on the blade, and Reed turned on the water to wash it off. He then left the bathroom, never seeing the naked, bloody body of Thi.

Downstairs he put the knife back where he had found it, figuring that he'd let the investigators search for the murder weapon—if they wanted it. A dead Vietnamese woman, one with a reputation of whoring around, probably wouldn't worry the Americans much. The South Vietnamese wouldn't care either. Just another dead whore.

He walked through the house one last time, looking for anything that could be traced directly back to him. Satisfied that no one would know he had been there, he let himself out, making sure that the door locked behind him.

As he reached the street and began to head toward the center of the town, the kids swarmed up, surrounding him. He grinned at them, tossed some coins off to one side and then hurried away. At the corner he stopped long enough to see that there were no adults visible. The adults would know that anything they saw would place them in jeopardy, so it was better never to see anything.

He walked along, feeling good. Maxwell had said that the leak had to be plugged and the soldiers would kill whoever was passing the information. He'd eliminated the biggest problem there. The only Vietnamese who could name him was dead.

He turned down a street, crossed to the other side and heard the first of the music coming from the bars. He walked through an alley, a filth-ridden area that stunk of rotting garbage and human waste. He heard a noise and jumped. The rat scurried for cover, disappearing into a rotting heap.

He laughed at himself and hurried forward into the brightness of the street. He stopped there and looked at the men and women around him. GIs with Vietnamese women. One man had the girl pushed into a dark alley, her skirt up around her hips, her panties around her knees. Reed joined a small group of men watching the two of them.

The GI finished and moved away, adjusting his clothes. As he turned, the men applauded. At first he was embarrassed, and then he bowed. The girl didn't seem to care. She had been paid for her time.

Reed hurried on, waved to a taxi and climbed into the rear, heading back to where he'd left his jeep. After he paid the man and got out, he then walked to the jeep and climbed behind the wheel.

His task was clear. He had to get back to MACV Headquarters. He unlocked the wheel and then sat there, staring at the sights around him. He thought about the GI and the girl and realized that it was the first time in his life that he had seen anything like that. Oh, he'd seen college boys and girls getting it on in the office or in the dormitory rooms where they came to sleep. One or two couples going at it in the semidarkness, not caring if the others in the room could see them. But this had been out on the street where a crowd watched.

The girl had been good-looking, though he hadn't seen that much of her face. Her hips, her legs and her bottom had looked good. Very good. For an instant he thought about heading back to see if he could find her, but then rejected the idea. For the next few weeks he'd have to be careful.

He pulled out into the traffic and headed toward MACV, slowing to wave at the MPs in one of the traffic posts. He made it back in record time and pulled into the lot. No one stopped him as he hurried into the building and down the stairs to the lower level. The MP there made him sign in again and then he walked on back to Maxwell's office where he knocked.

"Come."

Reed opened the door and found Maxwell sitting at his desk, working on a file.

"You got a few minutes?" asked Reed.

Maxwell dropped the report on his desk. "Sure," he replied.

Reed moved in and sat down in the visitor's chair. "I didn't want to say anything in front of those soldiers you had in here earlier. They didn't give me much of a chance."

"They're good men. Upset that someone opened his mouth and put them in jeopardy. You can trust them."

"On most things, probably, but not on this. Not after the way they went after me, and especially what you said they'd do to the leak." He leaned forward and said, "Which means I think I know where the leak is. Who it is."

Maxwell sat for a moment, stunned. He didn't know how to respond. It seemed too unlikely that Reed could have any idea, but then Maxwell didn't want to reject it outright before he heard it.

"Who?"

"Gary Pittman."

"That's shit. Pittman is so straight he squeaks when he walks."

"Not him, really," said Reed. "It's his girlfriend. He's got a Vietnamese girlfriend."

Maxwell sat up and stared. "So do half the men who work in this building."

That stopped Reed. "I met her once," he said. "A pretty woman."

"I'm afraid it isn't enough. That he has a Vietnamese girlfriend. There has to be more to it than that."

Reed looked at the floor, his mind racing. He had thought that walking in with the information would be enough to throw suspicion on Pittman. A man with a Vietnamese lover would be the logical person to suspect. He hadn't figured that everyone had a Vietnamese girlfriend.

"I heard she's a VC," said Reed.

Maxwell began to laugh. "If I had a dime for every time someone said that a Vietnamese was VC, I'd be a rich man and I wouldn't be working here."

Reed felt his anger flare. "I come in here with hot information about the possible leak and you blow it off. Don't give a shit about it."

"I didn't say that." Maxwell was still smiling. "I said rumors that someone is VC just aren't important. Besides, I would suspect that ten percent of the Vietnamese working in this building are VC."

"So we ignore the problem."

"No, I don't mean that either. But even if his girlfriend is a VC, it doesn't mean he's the leak."

Reed shook his head. "What do you want? A bomb set off under you. I'd say there's a good chance that I isolated the problem for you."

"Okay, Reed," said Maxwell. "Who is this girlfriend with ties to the VC?"

"Her name is Thi Vo Than."

"You know where she can be found?"

For a moment there was a picture flashing in his mind. The girl lying on her side, her legs pulled up, blood covering her, but he forced that image from his thoughts.

"No," he said. "I was only there once and I don't remember how we got there."

"All right," said Maxwell. "I'll check it out."

"When?"

"What the hell difference does that make?" asked Maxwell. "You in some kind of a hurry?"

"No." He started to say something more, but then decided against it.

Reed got up and said, "I think I better get going."

"Tomorrow," said Maxwell, "you be in here at seven. No more of this rolling in at midmorning shit."

Reed walked to the door and then stopped. He wanted to say something more, but couldn't think of how to phrase it. Anything more would sound like he was pushing too hard. Suspicion could slide from Pittman to him. He had to move carefully.

He walked out and found himself at loose ends. He didn't want to head to his quarters, because it was so damned depressing. He decided to drive back downtown and see if he could find the Vietnamese girl the GI had been with. The one with her panties around her knees.

With that thought he hurried to the gate, signed out and nearly ran to the parking lot. He liked the idea just fine.

KINSON HAD HOPED it would be simple to get from Tan Son Nhut to MACV Headquarters, but it turned into a chore. He didn't have any money because regulations suggested that wallets be left behind. Some men ignored that one. And no one wanted to carry loose change in the jungle.

Instead he had to try to bum a ride, and that was hard late in the day. Finally he found a jeep that had space in the back for him. He was dropped off out front and walked into the building. It took him several minutes to find out that Maxwell was still there, and then another several minutes to convince the MP that Maxwell would want to see him.

Maxwell appeared, walked forward and then stopped in his tracks. He stared at the man and finally said, "I thought you were dead."

Kinson shook his head. He still wore his dirty uniform, and hadn't showered. He had wanted to check in as soon as he could. "No, sir," he said flatly. "My patrol is dead, but I escaped."

Maxwell looked at the MP. "Open the gate."

The MP complied quickly and had Kinson sign in. Maxwell turned to the soldier. "I'll want to hear all about it."

"Yes, sir. I was—"

"Not here, Sergeant. In my office."

"Of course."

Maxwell regarded the MP with a stern look. "I don't want to be disturbed for the next hour or so."

"Yes, sir."

As they walked down the hall, Kinson felt the need to say something, anything. He wanted to fill his mind and forget about the bodies of his friends lying in the jungle. Trying to keep his voice light, he said, "I thought we had it rough, but you guys seem to work all the time."

"Not much to do around here but work," said Maxwell, opening the door. He glanced at Kinson, surprised by the comment, but then he'd dealt with many men who had just come in from the field, and they often said strange things. Many times the horrible truth hadn't set in. They were numb, talking almost as if to hear a human voice.

"Shit, sir," said Kinson, "I could find plenty to do."

Maxwell gestured and then sat down himself. "Anything you want?"

"Not now, sir. I'm fine."

"Okay. Well, now, in answer to your comment, if I'm not interested in drinking beer or chasing women, there isn't that much to do."

"But if you'd spent a week in the field, getting shot at, you'd want that beer."

"Granted," said Maxwell. He took a deep breath. "I've got a report from Gerber and Fetterman, a couple of Special Forces men I sent out after you. I know what happened to your patrol. In the grossest sense. You seemed to have walked into it."

Kinson ignored it. "Were they all dead?"

Maxwell lowered his voice. "I'm afraid so. We'll make arrangements to retrieve the bodies. Now, what happened to you?"

Kinson sat quietly for a moment before he replied. "They were waiting for us."

Maxwell nodded. "No question in your mind?"

"No, sir. They knew we were coming. There might have been several patrols out looking, waiting, but they knew that someone was coming, and we did nothing to clue them. They knew we were coming before we hit the field."

"What makes you say that?"

Kinson stared at Maxwell. He didn't speak for a moment. He felt the anger build through him. His fists clenched and his teeth clamped together, he finally said, his voice hard and metallic, "Some asshole here talked when he shouldn't have, and my men are dead."

"Sergeant," said Maxwell gently, "if I'm to catch the man or men responsible, I have to have your help. You must control your emotions and remain calm."

"Yes, sir."

"I'm going to have to ask you some hard questions. I don't want to, but I need the information." Maxwell leaned forward and touched the sergeant on the knee. "Okay?"

"Anything, sir, if it will help find the bastard."

"Think about this carefully. Was there any time, any place that you might have said something that could have been overheard? Is there a chance you might have said something that could have given away the mission?"

"No, sir," said Kinson immediately. "It's my butt that's hanging out. I know how to keep my mouth shut."

"Did you say anything to anyone here?"

"Only to your assistant. The man who briefed my team in the afternoon. We didn't say a word other than that." He stopped and snapped his fingers. "That helicopter crew knew where we were. At least where we started."

"But they wouldn't have had the chance to tell anyone. Besides, they only knew you were in South Vietnam, not that you were going to a town in Cambodia."

They talked about it for another thirty minutes. Maxwell examined it from all sides, trying to find an indication that Kinson or his men were somehow responsible, but knew he'd find nothing like that. The attack on Gerber's patrol told him that. Someone who had access to the data of both reports was the source of the leak. Kinson was right that the pilots had known the LZs, but not the final destination. They were clean. It had to be someone at MACV. An American at MACV.

When he finished, Maxwell stood up and asked, "You have a way to get back over to Tan Son Nhut?"

"No, sir."

Maxwell picked up a file folder and jammed it into his safe. He started to close it and then picked up the legal pad. He glanced at the names on it, trying to remember who would have known about both missions. Reed, of course. And Pittman, who was involved with the radio room and was responsible for the codes issued to the teams in the field. Hinsman might have known, but only because he was liaison between the Americans and the South Vietnamese. He would be a logical leak because of his position, but he wasn't sure that he had the information. Smith might have known, but it was unlikely.

As he ran down the list, he noticed that only a couple of names, Pittman and Reed, were definites. Reed and Pittman. Maxwell stuffed the pad into the drawer and locked it up. Maybe that limited where they had to look, and after all, Reed had been in telling him that Pittman's girlfriend was VC.

"Okay, Sergeant, I'm ready."

"I appreciate the lift, sir."

"No problem. You sure you want to return to Tan Son Nhut?"

"That's where all my gear is."

"Maybe you'd be better off staying downtown tonight."

Kinson laughed. A short bark. "I'll have to return to it sometime. Might as well be now."

"Up to you, Sergeant," said Maxwell. He followed the man out the door and locked it after them. Tomorrow might tell him who the traitor was. Tomorrow.

12

MACV HEADQUARTERS
SAIGON

It was still so early in the morning that the sun had yet to come up. Maxwell had taken his pistol, a Browning M-35 that had replaced the Swenson, from a locked desk drawer and tucked it into the shoulder holster he was now wearing. Shrugging on his suit coat, he headed for the door. He turned off the lights, locked the door and headed upstairs.

The others were sitting in a small conference room. The odor of coffee filled the air, almost masking the cigarette smoke. There were two other civilians present. One of them was Pittman and the other was Lawrence Talbott from the American embassy. He was a short, fleshy man with long hair and a beard—a thick, rich beard that Maxwell suspected was his statement about the establishment. He couldn't understand why anyone would wear a beard in the tropics if he wasn't making a statement.

Talbott sat at the table, his right foot on his left knee, which he kept in constant motion. Sweat covered his face, dripping down the sides. He looked hot and miserable as he smoked one cigarette after another, sipping coffee between puffs. He looked more annoyed than anything.

Pittman, on the other hand, looked scared. Like Talbott, he was sweating, but it was from nerves and not the heat. He tried to sit still and look calm, but he was failing badly. He kept glancing at Maxwell and then at the five MPs in the room. All were heavily armed, wore flak jackets and had brought shiny black helmet liners with large white 716s on them.

Maxwell looked at his watch, then at the captain in command of the MPs. "I'm ready, if you are, Captain."

The MP officer, John Layons, stabbed his cigarette into the brass shell-casing ashtray. He was a tall stocky man, who might have played football at one time. He looked tired. Black circles under his wide-set blue eyes, and a gray pallor under his tropical tan, showed how tired he was. His sandy-colored hair had been cut short, and there were beads of sweat in it, looking like drops of dew on the morning grass.

Layons turned his attention to Pittman. "Anything else we should know about the house?"

Pittman shook his head. "I told you everything I know." He looked at Talbott. "I didn't know she was a Vietcong. She was..."

"Nice?" Talbott finished for him with a sneer. "Friendly? Easy?"

Pittman fell silent for a moment, looking at Maxwell for help. He said, "I never told her a thing about the work. Never said a thing."

"We'll find out more about that later," snapped Talbott. "Right now, I'd suggest that you keep your mouth shut so you don't get yourself into more trouble."

Pittman looked at the MP officer, then at Maxwell, but didn't speak. He looked as if he was on the verge of tears. The rich boy who had bought one too many beers and now found himself in front of the sheriff, charged with reckless driving.

Maxwell said, "Let's get going."

"Certainly." Layons pointed at Pittman. "You'll ride in the first jeep with Sergeant Burns. You'll show us the way. Once we get there, you'll stay in the jeep until we call for you."

"Yes, sir."

"Everyone clear on his assignment?"

The MPs nodded. Sergeant Burns said, "Once we're there, I take Smith around to the back and wait until I hear you enter the front, then go in the back."

"Right."

Layons drained his coffee and set it on the table. The others did the same and then headed for the door. They filed out of the room, down the hall and through the double doors that took them outside. The night was still muggy. There were hundreds of insects swarming around the light poles. Layons waved at the MP on guard in the tiny shack closer to the street.

They piled into three jeeps, each with blackout covers on the headlights. The last vehicle had an M-16 mounted in the rear for a little extra firepower in case they needed it. Burns drove the first jeep with Pittman sitting stiffly in the seat beside him.

As he started the engine, Layons leaned closer to Maxwell. "What do you think?"

"He didn't know she was VC, so he could be the leak, but he'd have to be incredibly stupid to tell her about patrols going out and that sort of thing. I don't like it."

"But the woman is on our list of suspected enemy agents."

"Still doesn't mean that Pittman is the leak."

They headed out, entering the streets of Saigon. Like Las Vegas, Saigon was a city that never slept. The neon signs above the bars were lurid, and the rock music from live bands and tape recorders still blared. People jammed the streets. GIs trying to cram as much living into a three-day pass as they could. Women, trying to siphon as much money from those GIs as they could. If it hadn't been dark, Maxwell would have thought it midday. There were hundreds of people. Thousands.

They passed through the area and into the residential neighborhoods. It was quiet there, with only the occasional bark of a dog. The odor that was sometimes blown away by the afternoon breezes hung in the air like a curtain. It was a foul odor of too many people shoved into too small a space.

They turned again and came to a street with a row of neat houses. Small structures built by the French and owned by some of the more affluent Vietnamese.

"She's doing all right for herself," said Maxwell.

Layons didn't reply.

The lead jeep pulled to the side of the street. Pittman pointed at a house, and Burns nodded. Layons pulled up right behind them and the third jeep stopped in the middle of the street. One of the MPs climbed up behind the M-60.

Without a word, Burns and another man got out and ran around to the side of the house. They halted near the short wall there, hesitated and then climbed to the top. A moment later they both disappeared.

Layons moved to the lead jeep, leaned close to Pittman and told him to remain right there. Then he, with two others and Maxwell, headed toward the front of the house. Talbott grabbed Maxwell. "Shouldn't we have a warrant?"

"Hell," said Maxwell, "we should have a local representative with us, but then we'd lose our chance. We'd lose the element of surprise."

"Meaning?"

Maxwell rolled his eyes and didn't answer. He moved forward to join up with Layons. He pulled his pistol from under his coat. Layons had a CAR-15, and the MPs with them carried M-16s. They spread out along the front of the house, one man covering the main window and another taking a position to cover the man moving to the front door.

Layons raised a foot to kick, but Maxwell stopped him. He leaned close and said, "A little finesse goes a long way." He reached into his pocket and brought out a small leather case. "Let me."

Layons pointed at the lock and said, "Go right ahead."

Maxwell holstered his pistol and then unzipped his case. He pulled out a straight probe and one that had a slight hook on the end. Crouching in front of the lock, Maxwell inserted one probe and then the other, working to push the tumblers up and out of the way. He worked on the lock, twisting the probes until the lock clicked open. He looked up at Layons and grinned.

As he stepped out of the way, he put his tools back in their case and pulled his pistol, while Layons moved forward and took hold of the knob. He turned it slowly and then pushed on the door. It swung open quietly.

Layons entered the house, stopping just inside the door. He tried to remember the diagram that Pittman had made. A living room to the right and a hallway to the left that led into the kitchen. Bedrooms upstairs.

Pointing at one of his men and then at the living room, Layons moved to the stairs. He turned and sent another man toward the rear of the house. Clear the downstairs and then move to the second floor.

Maxwell joined him at the foot of the stairs. One MP appeared and held up a thumb. The second did the same, and Layons started to move up. Again Maxwell stopped him and leaned very close.

"Use the sides, and step on the front of the riser. Less chance of noise."

Layons stared at him but moved to the side, taking Maxwell's advice. He flattened himself against the wall as he slowly climbed the steps. Maxwell, his pistol in his right hand locked against his shoulder, followed. They reached the top of the stairs and stopped. Maxwell caught the odor first. Hot copper. He glanced at Layons who shrugged.

They moved into the bedroom. Layons slid around the door and then crouched, his back to the wall, using the shadows to hide. Maxwell moved right to the bed. He aimed at the center of it, and although it was unmade, he could tell that the tangle of sheets and pillows did not conceal a body.

Layons swept a flashlight beam around the room. They found nothing out of place. Then Layons slipped into the hallway, moving toward the bathroom. Maxwell was right behind him. The odor was stronger, now.

As they reached the door, Maxwell reached out to stop Layons. He leaned very close. "Don't touch anything."

Again the MP was annoyed. He didn't like the spook telling him his job. Still, he was careful to avoid touching any surface that might have taken a print.

This time he didn't enter the room. Using the wall for protection, he snapped on the light. In a flash he saw the gore-covered body of the woman. He turned the light off again and looked away, gulping at the air. He was used to seeing violent death, but not that of naked young women.

Maxwell wasn't sure what he had seen. From the odor hanging in the hallway, he thought he knew what Layons had seen. He took the light from the MP's hand and turned it on. He looked at the puddled blood, the splatters that dripped down the wall, and the crusting blood around the body.

"Been dead for a while," said Maxwell speaking in a normal tone of voice.

That caught Layons off guard for a moment. "Yeah. Better get Pittman up here," he finally said.

"Don't tell him what we've found. Let's see his reaction to the body."

Layons turned on Maxwell. "How about you stop telling me how to handle my job?"

"Sorry."

One of the MPs peeked around the corner of the staircase. "Everything all right up here, Captain?"

"You go get Mr. Pittman and tell him we want to make sure we've got the right woman."

"Yes, sir."

Layons stepped into the bathroom, one foot in the door. He stopped then, not wanting to spoil the evidence. Again he used his flashlight, spotted the light switch and used the muzzle of his weapon to punch it. He turned and saw the full horror of the blood-caked body.

"Oh my God," he said. "Jesus."

Maxwell centered himself in the door and looked at the dead woman. He told himself that she was an enemy agent, working to see Americans killed, but that didn't lessen the impact of seeing the body. No one deserved to die like that.

There was a noise behind them. Maxwell stepped away and walked down the hall. He found a light switch and snapped it on. That made the light streaming from the bathroom less noticeable.

Pittman was climbing the stairs. He stopped halfway and asked, "What's going on?"

"We want to make sure that we've captured the right woman here."

Pittman started up again. Maxwell stepped in front of him so that he couldn't see anything of the bathroom. When they were close to the door, he stepped aside and then turned to look at Pittman's face.

Pittman started forward, a hand in front of him. "Thi," he said, "I'm sorry, but they believe you're..." He stopped dead in his tracks. The color drained from his face. His eyes began to roll up into his head and his knees buckled.

Maxwell leaped forward and caught the man as he fell. He lowered the body to the floor. "Looks like he was caught by surprise," said Maxwell.

"Either that or he's one hell of an actor."

One of the MPs said, "I'll get some water," and started for the bathroom. He saw the body then and gasped, "Jesus Christ." He turned away. "What in hell happened?"

"She was murdered," said Maxwell.

"He do it?"

"I don't think so."

Pittman groaned and opened his eyes. He pulled away from Maxwell. "Oh, Jesus Christ, what did you people do to her?"

"That's the way we found her."

"Oh Jesus," he said again and then gulped rapidly, as if he were about to throw up. "Oh Jesus, oh Jesus. What happened?"

"You feel well enough to stand?" asked Maxwell.

Pittman got to his feet and wobbled there. Maxwell held on to him and motioned the MP over. "You take Gary out and get him some fresh air."

"Yes, sir."

"Then you get the others together and—"

"If you don't mind, Mr. Maxwell, I'll handle this," Layons blurted.

"By all means."

Layons, who looked like he had regained his composure, stepped forward. "Radio this in to Waco and have then get someone from the local police force here. Tell them to hurry and that we'll preserve the crime scene until they arrive. We have no suspects yet."

"We're going to have to tell them why we're here, and that's going to blow my investigation out of the water."

"I don't see how. Your boy already knows that we're on to him. He served up the girl as a source, hoping to draw heat off himself."

"Still, we don't have to tell them everything at this moment," said Maxwell. "We get a good answer, we can always hand it to them, but I don't want to lose my guy to them."

Layons said, "Just tell them to get someone here and that we'll stay until they arrive. Nothing else."

"Yes, sir."

"And tell our guys not to talk to them at all. They don't know a thing."

"Yes, sir."

While Layons gave instructions to the other MPs, Maxwell moved forward and stared into the bathroom. It hadn't been a simple murder. There had been frenzied activity involved. From five or six feet away, he couldn't be sure, but it looked like some of the wounds were ragged, as if the knife had been twisted. A crime of passion. The murderer had wanted to destroy the victim, not just kill her.

He backed away and shook his head. Maybe the VC had learned that she was burned as a source and had killed her. Or maybe it was as Layons suggested. The leak gave her up as the source, trying to divert the suspicion.

He walked down the stairs and out into the night. The sky was beginning to turn gray with the coming of the sun. He looked up at the fading stars and wondered how someone could kill like that. It seemed to be an impossible thing, even in a war zone, but it wasn't. And that's what worried him.

13

**CARASEL HOTEL
DOWNTOWN SAIGON**

Gerber couldn't sleep. He was up and down all night. He turned on the tiny black-and-white television, but unlike the World, where the bigger cities sometimes showed all-night movies, AFVN shut down as soon as Carson, or one of the other late-night shows, was over. Nothing to watch, when it would be the perfect time to stay up with a Bogart classic.

Morrow wasn't having a similar problem. She had fallen asleep immediately and had hardly stirred. Not even Gerber's bumping into the wardrobe had awakened her.

He got the Beam's out, took it into the bathroom and made himself a drink, using some cold water with the alcohol. He hoped that no one ever discovered that he sometimes weakened the drink with water. He returned to the bedroom and opened the curtain so that he could look down on the streets of Saigon.

As always, he was surprised that there were people moving around. It didn't make any difference what time it was, there would always be people on the street.

He turned away from the window and stared into the gloom of his room. Morrow was a vague shape under the sheet, one foot sticking out where he could grab it, if he decided it was time for her to wake up.

But that wasn't the reason he was awake. It was the damned leak at MACV. No pressure on the brass hats and other pukes who worked there. They weren't the ones going into the field to be ambushed. Only the men who had to fight the war had to worry. Someone was selling, hell, maybe giving secrets to the enemy, and it had to be an American. There was no way for the Vietnamese to have access to some of the data.

That's what Maxwell had said, and Maxwell should know. An American doing it to his fellows. Gerber shook his head and looked at his watch. It was too early to do anything about it now. Later in the day he could start to work on the problem, but now anyone with half a brain was asleep.

Gerber chuckled to himself, because he must have half a brain. He couldn't sleep. Just no way. He drained the last of the Beam's in his glass and set it on top of the air conditioner. He moved to the wardrobe, opened it and took out a clean uniform. With his right hand, he found his holstered M-35 pistol and took it out too.

Trying not to waken Morrow, though she seemed to be so deeply asleep he could open fire and not wake her, he walked to the bathroom. He closed the door and turned on the light. Quickly he dressed, saw that he should shave and decided that it wouldn't make that much difference.

After tiptoeing out to the hall with his boots in his hand, Gerber put them on and went down to the lobby where, much to his surprise, he found Fetterman.

"Couldn't sleep," explained the master sergeant.

"Yeah. Me either."

"I was trying to think of a way of calling you without waking Robin. Thought I'd try ESP."

Gerber grinned. "Did it work?"

"You're here, sir. You figure it out."

Gerber pointed at the front door. "Want to head over to MACV and see what's cooking there?"

"My thoughts exactly." Fetterman checked the time. It was just before five. "Might be a little early for them."

"So we steal doughnuts and drink coffee. There'll be someone on watch over there."

"Works for me," said Fetterman.

Together they walked out into the humidity of the city. It was still hot, even that early in the morning. Gerber felt the sweat bead immediately.

Fetterman walked to the curb, saw a taxi and waved at it. The driver eased on over and slipped up to the curb.

Fetterman opened the rear door and Gerber climbed in. The driver looked at them and asked, "Where to, Joe?"

"MACV."

The driver nodded and checked the traffic before pulling into traffic.

They rode in silence through the darkened streets until they came to the blazing MACV headquarters. A VC gunner with a mortar tube would have no trouble identifying the target, but that rarely happened. The mortars and rockets dropped on Saigon to frighten the civilians. The military targets were avoided.

Fetterman paid the driver, and the two men walked up to the building. There were some lights on in some of the offices. Sergeants and lieutenants getting ready for the day. As they entered, there were some people moving about. Men in uniform, khakis or jungle fatigues, but no women. The Vietnamese wouldn't show up for another several hours.

"Think Maxwell's in?" asked Fetterman.

"If he's smart, he's not. Let's go look."

They walked downstairs to the iron gate where a tired MP sat, trying desperately to stay awake. He stood as Gerber approached.

"Maxwell in?"

The MP looked at the sign-in sheets. "Nope. Left about an hour ago."

Gerber looked at Fetterman. "How about that? If we'd hurried, we'd have got him." Then turning to the MP he said, "Thanks. You see him, tell him that Captain Gerber is in the building and would like to talk with him."

"Yes, sir."

They headed back upstairs. "Let's see if we can find those doughnuts," suggested Fetterman.

As they reached the top of the stairs, they saw Reed enter the building. He looked as if he had been out all night. His clothes were dirty and the sleeve of his shirt was torn. He glanced at Gerber and Fetterman and then beyond them, as if he didn't see them.

Gerber looked at Fetterman and whispered, "Maybe God does like us."

"You know his name?"

"Reed."

Gerber moved toward the man and said, "Hey, Reed, we talk to you for a minute?"

Reed looked at him. "I'm heading down to see Jerry. Check in with him."

"Jerry's not there," said Gerber. "We just came from there."

"Well then, what do you want?"

Gerber glanced back. "Let's move into the conference room down here so we won't be disturbed."

"Sounds serious," Reed said, trying to sound casual.

But Gerber insisted. "Come on."

They walked down the hall to the conference room. Fetterman opened the door and turned on the lights. As he did, he whispered to Gerber, "I'll tell the MP to send Maxwell up here when he gets in."

"Good idea." Gerber stepped in and took a seat close to the door. He pointed at the head of the table. "Have a seat. I don't think I know your first name."

"Philip."

"Have a seat, Philip." Gerber rocked back and laced his fingers behind his head. It had been simple to maneuver it so that Reed would have to pass him to get out. Saved a hassle if Reed decided he didn't like the questions.

As he sat down, Reed asked, "Where'd the sergeant go?"

"Went in search of coffee. Find us something to get our hearts started."

Reed sat there but didn't respond. Gerber stared at him, but the younger man didn't get uncomfortable, didn't squirm in his chair. Finally Gerber leaned forward, his elbows on the edge of the table.

"Got a couple of questions for you."

"All right. Remember, though, I don't have access to everything around here."

"Understood." Gerber studied the man's eyes. They seemed to be flat, dead, as if there were no soul to the man. Once again Gerber realized how much he didn't like Reed. There was something about him that Gerber couldn't stomach, and if anyone had asked him why, he wouldn't have had an answer.

"You know," said Gerber, "that we've got a problem here. Someone talking out of turn."

"Mr. Maxwell and I have been working on it."

"Yes," said Gerber. "You have any ideas on how the information is getting out? You know who might be leaking it to the VC?"

"I spoke to Jerry about it last evening. Gave him everything I knew then. You want to know, maybe you should wait for him to get back."

"Why not fill me in now? Save us time later on. Jerry and I have no secrets."

"I don't know about that. We're talking about a leak, and you want me to leak information to you."

Before Gerber could respond, the door opened and Fetterman entered.

"Where's the coffee?" asked Reed.

"He couldn't find any," Gerber replied harshly.

Fetterman crossed his arms and leaned back against the door. He didn't say anything.

The captain turned his attention back to Reed. "Now, I was wondering what you told Maxwell."

Reed stared at Gerber, then at Fetterman. "Are you threatening me?"

Gerber laughed. "Threatening you? What in the hell makes you think that?"

"The way your sergeant comes and leans on the door there."

"If I wanted to threaten you, I wouldn't need Sergeant Fetterman's help. Now, let's get back to the issue. What did you tell Maxwell?"

Sweat had blossomed on Reed's forehead. He wiped at it, then rubbed his hand on the thigh of his pants. "Not much to tell him, really."

"Then you won't mind telling me."

"I guess it can't hurt," said Reed. His voice was higher, as if he were scared. His eyes shifted right and left. He leaned forward and lowered his voice.

"I found out that Gary Pittman, one of the other new guys around here, had a girlfriend in town. She's a VC, and Pittman has been spending a lot of time with her."

Gerber snorted. "That's shit. Every other Vietnamese is VC. Hell, half the people who work here are probably VC."

"That's what Maxwell said."

"He going to check it out?"

"Well," said Reed, "what do you think? I'll bet they do, but it won't do them any good. The girl's dead. Pittman must have done it so that he could get off. He'll probably be reassigned in the next couple of days.''

"You seem to know a lot about Pittman's business," said Fetterman.

"Well," said Reed, "after I learned that we were having trouble, I started keeping my eyes open. I knew that Pittman had a girlfriend, so I asked around."

"How do you know she's VC?" asked Fetterman.

"Talked to some of the Vietnamese here. They told me. Had to be very careful about it, though. Didn't want them to know why I wanted to know. Had to talk around it until one of them let it drop that she was VC. Once I learned that, I knew who the leak was."

"Why?" asked Gerber.

"Because Pittman has a big mouth. Likes to hear himself talk. I can see him now, sitting there with her, telling her about what's happening at work. Little things about the patrols and such. Then she runs off and tells her VC bosses." Reed twisted his face up like he had gotten a whiff of something soft and warm and smelly. "He'd just be bragging about what he knew, and she was listening oh so carefully, and the next thing you know, our boys are dead in the jungle."

Gerber glanced at Fetterman and then asked, "How do you know this?"

"Oh, I don't know for sure. I suspect it, though. It would be like Pittman, wanting to prove what an important man he is. Talking away, never thinking about what he was saying. Just that he was important because he had the inside scoop on everything."

"So you think we don't have to look any farther than Pittman." Gerber was amazed that Reed, who had been reluctant to talk at first, now wouldn't shut up.

"That's what I think. Oh, he'll deny it, but you know and I know that it has to be Pittman. No one else it could be."

There was a knock at the door. Gerber glanced at Fetterman who opened it and stepped out.

"Anything else?" asked Gerber.

Now Reed laughed. "What more do you want? We all know that it was Pittman."

Gerber sat there, elbows on the table, and said nothing. There was something else about the man that Gerber didn't like. Maybe it was the way he was so sure that Pittman had to be the source of the leak. Maybe it was the way he stared Gerber in the eyes as if to prove how honest he was.

"Maxwell's here," Fetterman announced from the doorway.

Gerber stood up. "Well, I guess that covers it. You going to be around here for the rest of the day?"

"I work here. I'll be around."

Gerber moved to the door, but Reed didn't budge. Gerber glanced at him, and then opened the door, and when he saw the look on Maxwell's face, asked, "What in the hell happened to you?"

Maxwell pulled out a handkerchief and mopped his face with it. "Let's go down to my office. We can talk in there."

Gerber nodded at the door. "Reed's sitting in there, waiting for you."

"We can talk to him later."

They all went downstairs, stopping at the gate to sign in. They moved through it, but before they went too far, Maxwell stopped. He looked at the MP. "Could you see if you could scare up some Cokes for us?"

The MP was about to tell Maxwell that he wasn't a servant, but then he saw the look on Maxwell's face. He said, "Might take a few minutes, I can't leave my post."

"I know that," said Maxwell. "Just see what you can do for us."

"Yes, sir."

They then continued down the hall and Maxwell unlocked his door. He pushed it open, entered and turned on the light. Moving directly to the chair, he sat down and glanced at Gerber. "How do you stand it?"

"Stand what?"

"The butcher's yard. The blood and the gore splattered all over everywhere."

"You don't stand it," said Fetterman. "You get immune to seeing it, you control your emotions, but you don't stand it. You still see the broken, ruined bodies, and you still smell the odor of death. It no longer makes you physically sick, but it's always there in the background, reminding you what war is about."

"Christ, I've never seen anything like this."

"Like what?" asked Gerber.

"That poor woman. Cut up and lying in her own blood in the bathroom. A real sadistic son of a bitch got at her. Wasn't happy with just killing her."

"The Vietcong are famous for that," said Gerber. "Killing someone isn't enough. They have to send a message to everyone who sees the body."

"We thought we had the man, the leak. Brought him out there to confront the woman. Pittman walked right in without blinking an eye."

"Pittman do it?" asked Fetterman.

"I don't think so," said Maxwell. "As I say, he walked in without blinking, but then it seemed that he expected to talk to her. He was as surprised as the rest of us. Passed out when he saw her, and thinking back on it, he said absolutely nothing that suggested he knew she was dead."

"Could Pittman be the source of the leak, and now that he's burned, the VC killed the woman?"

Maxwell closed his eyes and squeezed the bridge of his nose. "I wouldn't think so. No reason for the VC to kill her, even if

Pittman is the leak. They could move her to Nha Trang or Da Nang or a dozen other places and put her to work again.''

"That leaves Pittman,'' said Gerber.

"I don't think so,'' said Maxwell. "Pittman isn't that dumb. He might have been fooling around with the woman—hell, probably was—but that doesn't mean a thing. We don't even know if she was VC.''

"I thought that had been established,'' said Gerber.

"Nothing's established yet except that the woman is dead. The MPs and the local police are trying to piece together the information now.''

There was a knock and Maxwell yelled, "Come.''

The MP opened the door and held up the three cans of Coke. Maxwell smiled slightly. "You may have just saved my life.''

Fetterman took the cans and passed them out. As the MP retreated, Maxwell opened his can and drank deeply. He set the can down and took a deep breath.

"We're back to where we started,'' said Maxwell.

"Not necessarily,'' Gerber countered. "You say that you don't think Pittman is the source. We've got a dead woman, and I'll bet money that if we find the source of the leak, we find the killer.''

"There isn't much in the evidence at the scene,'' said Maxwell. "Oh, one thing. The man was cold. He took a shower after he did it. Cleaned himself up before he left.'' Maxwell shook his head. "Cut her up and left her lying there while he cleaned himself.''

"Got a murder weapon?''

"No. A knife, but hell, what's that mean? How many knives you have?''

Gerber shrugged. "Normally carry one. I could get another dozen without any trouble. Those survival knives, blades about six inches long are all over the place.''

"My point exactly,'' said Maxwell. "No way to trace it even if we did have it.''

Fetterman crushed his empty Coke can. "We got to move quickly. Whoever it is has got to know that we're out here looking for him. He's going to fold his tent and strike his colors."

"Then we've accomplished half the mission," said Maxwell. "We've stopped him effectively. He'll still have access, but he won't be able to pass it."

"Not enough," said Gerber. "While he's free, he's still a threat. Besides, he's responsible for the deaths of several Americans. Stopping him isn't enough. We've got to identify him."

"And then what?" asked Maxwell. "Kill him?"

Gerber hesitated. "Probably."

14

MACV HEADQUARTERS
SAIGON

Reed couldn't believe the sudden rush of relief that came over him. He was sure that Gerber was going to order him arrested, but that didn't happen. Gerber had left the room without a word. When Reed had told him that he had work to do, Gerber had assumed that he was going to stay at MACV headquarters. Reed knew that it was too late for that. He had to get out. It seemed everything was closing in on him.

As soon as the hallway was clear, Reed entered and walked to the front door. Gerber, his pet master sergeant and Maxwell would be downstairs for an hour or more. That would give him the time he would need.

He hurried down the sidewalk and across the parking lot to where he'd left his jeep. He climbed behind the wheel and then sat there for a moment, waiting and watching. He was sure that someone would come flying out of the building after him, and he didn't want them to think he was running away if they did appear.

Finally he started the engine and drove out, forcing himself to keep it slow because he didn't want to call attention to himself. He glanced over his shoulder and saw the MP in the guard shack step out into the sunlight, but the man just stretched his arms over his head. No one was paying the slightest attention to Reed.

He drove downtown through the growing mass of people who were coming out of the buildings and filling the streets. Ants moving in response to some unseen, unheard command. Reed grinned at the stupid people, moving through their lives while others made the decisions that affected them. Others decided who would live and who would die. And they weren't even smart enough to realize it. They thought they controlled their own destiny.

He finally reached the downtown hotel, off the beaten path, that he used as a base. A five-story job, the front streaked with rust from the gutters around the red tile roof. High windows that were nearly opaque because of decades of dirt. The small building offered cheap rooms and cheap women. A few enlisted men also lived there. Reed knew he could hide from the brass hats and the political animals who haunted the first-rate hotels and the MACV headquarters.

Reed locked his jeep and entered the small and dingy lobby. The floor, which once might have been magnificent, was covered with years of grime. The desk at the far end had a hole in the front where an angry GI had kicked it. A potted palm had died and no one had bothered to take it out. Two men slept on the floor, off to one side, and a Vietnamese woman wearing the world's shortest skirt sat near them like a dog guarding her master.

Reed walked across the lobby to the stairs and took them two at a time to the third floor. The hallway there was nearly pitch black. A window at the far end permitted just enough light that he could walk down the hall without tripping over the sleeping man or the single table. He pulled a key out of his pocket, unlocked the door, and entered his hideaway.

The room was hot and humid, stinking of vomit, urine and sweat. The last tenant had been a fat sergeant who drank himself unconscious nearly every night and rarely made the bathroom when he was sick. He'd lived with a Vietnamese woman who tried to clean up after him, but who didn't understand the finer points of running water and flush toilets. Besides, the water was intermittent, and the toilet refused to flush half the time.

There was a single bed, a chair with a broken leg and an electric light hanging from a bare wire. But it was cheap and no one knew he had it.

Reed moved to the window and forced it open, hoping for a cool breeze where there was none. Only the sounds of the city and a cloud of diesel fumes and city dust. Having opened the window, he turned and was sure that he was going to have to run. It was all coming apart now. They were after him.

Then he remembered again that they didn't know about the room. His safehouse. He sat down in the chair and closed his eyes. Safe for the moment.

Not that the dummies would figure out what was going on in the near future. Gerber had scared him because it seemed that Gerber knew he was the leak. The captain seemed to sense it, but couldn't prove it, so he had left Reed alone. Gerber had given him the chance to escape.

Reed laughed out loud. "Those assholes," he said. They'd never catch him. They were as dumb as Thi. She had thought she was pumping him for information. Oh, she had been pumping him, that was certain, but it wasn't for information. She'd climb on board and take a ride, and then he'd let it drop that someone was patrolling in Tay Ninh, someone was searching for the supply base of the enemy, or whatever, and she wouldn't be able to wait for him to leave. Thought that he didn't know. Hell, everyone knew. He was making it a game for her, but it was one played by his rules.

He stood up and moved to the window. With a hand on either side of the frame, he leaned his forehead against the dirty glass and listened to the sounds of Saigon, while images played through his head. First Thi lying in her own blood because she was no longer useful to him alive, and then the Vietnamese woman who had spent the night with him. A young woman, no more than eighteen, though she said she was fourteen. Another lie for the sick GI mind. Tell them you were young and they paid more for it.

But she had been willing and she had been limber. She had done everything he had wanted and then hoped to flee into the night with a fistful of money. Reed didn't care about the money. Not now, anyway. But he couldn't let her go, knowing about his secret room. She was a threat to him and had to die. A survival knife, picked up at MACV had done the trick easily and silently. She'd barely groaned as she died.

He walked over to the rickety nightstand and pulled out a notepad. He returned to the chair, sat down and started to write a letter. A note really, telling Thom that it was finally all over. He had pushed it too far too fast and now they were coming to get him.

"But don't worry about me," he wrote. "I know how to avoid them. Thi told me, never realizing that she told me. She talked about spending her afternoons, when I or Gary Pittman weren't around, at the Cercle Raquette. When I'm finished here, I'll go over there and arrange to get out of Vietnam somehow."

He stopped writing and wondered if he should tell his friend what it had been like to kill the girl. About the power he felt as the knife plunged into her. He understood about power now, and manipulation, but killing someone might be an abstraction his friend didn't fully comprehend. In the end he decided against it. When he returned to the States, if Thom was the man he remembered him to be, and if they were both drunk enough or stoned enough, he might tell him. But not until then.

There were so many things that he wanted to tell Thom. He'd learned so much since they had shared the basement office in Berkeley. He'd moved so far beyond the theories they had discussed. He knew how to use the system now. He could make it work for him, make it carry out his plans, and when things went wrong, knew how to shift the blame to someone else. He had more power than most people dreamed about.

He looked up from his writing pad, at the body of the Vietnamese woman lying in his bed. She had died easier than Thi. He learned something there too. Learned that the blood wasn't necessary for the woman to die. A knife in the right place could paralyze the heart. He didn't have to slash at the victim to kill her. There was some blood, but not the puddles of it that Thi had created.

Looking back at the letter, he decided that he'd better finish it. It was time to get out of the room and out of Vietnam. The others might be stupid, but they would eventually figure out what had happened.

Speaking out loud, as if to a superior, he said, "But it wasn't my fault. I had to act quickly. There had been no time to plan things carefully."

He folded the letter and put it into an envelope. He set that aside and moved to the bed, sitting on the edge. He stared at the dead woman, the single wound in her chest just under her breastbone. Blood had flowed from the wound, down her belly to spread over the sheets between her legs. He patted her bare thigh, the skin cold and unyielding. Just like all women, he thought.

"It's time to get out," he told her. He stood up, took his pistol from under the mattress where he hid it, and walked to the door.

GERBER SAT IN THE CHAIR, sipped his Coke and looked at the bare walls in Maxwell's office. Finally he pointed and said, "Where the hell are your Indian fighter pictures?"

"Frames kept getting broken. I took them down."

"Well shit," said Fetterman. "I liked that Wagon Box Fight one."

Maxwell looked at Fetterman and asked, "Why?"

"My great-grandfather, William Fetterman, once bragged that he could ride through the whole Sioux Nation with eighty good men. He tried one winter day in 1866, and forty minutes later all eighty good men were dead. Some say he killed himself to keep from being captured by the Indians, and others say he died in the fighting."

"What's that got to do with the Wagon Box Fight?"

"The following August," said Fetterman, "Captain James Powell, facing a large force of Sioux, drove them off and became the hero of the Wagon Box Fight. That was the same Captain Powell who was supposed to rescue a woodcutting party until my grandfather pulled rank on him and rode out to his doom."

"Which has nothing to do with the problem at hand," said Maxwell.

"No, Jerry, but it's an interesting story."

"Sure. Interesting."

Gerber stood up and walked toward the door, then over to the file cabinets and finally back to his chair. He looked at Maxwell and said, "It has got to be Reed. It's got to be."

"What do you have to go on?" asked Maxwell. "Other than your dislike for him and a gut feeling."

"The man is too quick to point the finger at others. First tries to give up the Cambodians who are dead and unable to defend themselves, and when that fails, gives us Pittman."

"Whose girlfriend was VC," said Maxwell.

"According to Reed. Now she's conveniently dead, too."

"But Reed couldn't know she was dead," said Maxwell. "No way for him to know it, because we didn't know it until we'd found the body. I came directly from the scene to MACV."

Gerber sat bolt upright and glanced at Fetterman. "What did you say?"

"I came here from the scene." Maxwell raised his eyebrows in question.

"No. Before that. You said that Reed couldn't know the woman was dead because you hadn't gotten back yet."

Maxwell still didn't understand. "The MPs knew and they passed the word to Waco, their control, to get the local police, but nothing about the reason."

Gerber slapped the arm of his chair. "Got him!"

"What?"

Gerber looked at Maxwell and said, "While you were finding the body of the woman, Reed was upstairs telling me that Pittman must have killed her."

Suddenly Maxwell understood. "The only way he could know the woman was dead was if he'd . . ."

"Killed her," Gerber finished for him. "Exactly."

Maxwell pulled his pistol from his shoulder holster and looked at it. "Then let's go upstairs and have a chat with Mr. Reed. I have some very hard questions for him."

REED WALKED OUT of the hotel and onto the hot street. He stood there a moment, blinking, sure that he had forgotten something but couldn't recall what it might be. There was nothing upstairs except for the dead woman. Nothing that belonged to him, and the Vietnamese clerk had been only too happy to take the ten dollars rather than see an ID card.

In his real room at the Carasel, there was everything he owned in Vietnam. Clothes, books and magazines, but nothing that couldn't be easily replaced. No reason to go there.

He looked at the street, at the people swirling around him without a purpose. He moved to the curb and raised a hand. He shouted at a taxi and the cab slowed, coming toward him.

"Where?"

Reed shrugged, thought about a change of clothes, a hotel shower and a few minutes to relax. "Carasel Hotel."

They drove across town and as they did, Reed suddenly remembered that he had a jeep. He could have driven himself, but it didn't matter now. If the Army found it, it would just keep them busy in the wrong place that much longer. In a couple of hours he would be on his way out of Vietnam.

At the Carasel he paid the driver and walked across the large, bright lobby. It was quite a contrast to the hole-in-the-wall where he sometimes hid. He nodded to the Vietnamese behind the desk and continued on. He saw a striking American woman, blond hair, tall, slender, coming at him and nodded to her.

"Good morning."

She looked surprised, said, "Good morning," and kept on going.

Reed used the elevator to the fourth floor and hurried down the hallway. At the door he fumbled with his keys, unlocked it and entered. As he did, he was suddenly uneasy. It was stupid coming here. It would be the first place they would look if they tumbled to him, but he still wasn't convinced that the trail would lead to him.

He turned on the air conditioner and then the radio tuned to AFVN. They were playing the latest rock and roll. Or rather the latest they had, which was about six months behind what was happening in the World.

For a moment he listened to it and then stripped, moving into the bathroom. He turned on the shower and then looked at himself in the mirror. There was a ragged red stain on his chest. Blood from the woman he'd killed the night before.

Now he began to laugh. That Army dickhead sitting across the table from him, talking about leaks and traitors and who they might hang for it, and he was sitting there, the blood of his last victim still on his chest. A large ragged oval of dried blood. It was a shame to wash it off, but he had to do it.

He stepped into the shower, adjusted it until it was warm and began to soap himself. Maybe he had time for one more woman before he escaped. One more chance to feel the power.

NATURALLY when they reached the conference room, Reed was gone. "It would have been too easy if he'd been here," said Gerber.

Maxwell rubbed his hands anxiously. "Now all we have to do is figure out where he might have gone."

"If we were the police," said Fetterman, "we'd start with his room and work it from there."

"Of course," said Gerber. "Jerry, you got a jeep?"

"Yeah, come on." They headed out to the parking lot and Maxwell unlocked the wheel. "How we going to handle this?" he asked.

"We take him quickly and then drag him over to the MP headquarters. Turn him in there," said Gerber.

"Captain," Fetterman said, "maybe he should die in the shoot-out."

"What shoot-out?" asked Maxwell.

Gerber turned to face Fetterman who was sitting in the back of the jeep. "We go in, tell him we know he's the leak, the spy working for the enemy. He draws on us."

"What shoot-out?" repeated Maxwell.

Fetterman continued, oblivious to the CIA man. "We have to open up. We don't want to do it, but he gives us no choice. We have to do it. It's him or us."

"As long as the physical evidence backs us up on this," said Gerber.

Maxwell looked at the two of them. "You remember the trouble you got into over the Chinese guy. Court-martials and all."

"That was different," said Gerber. "That was an assassination attempt on a foreign national. This is an arrest of a spy.

One responsible for the deaths of a number of American soldiers.''

Maxwell said, ''Let me go first. I want to see him arrested and in jail. Give me that much.''

''Jerry, he's responsible for the deaths of American soldiers. He killed an unarmed woman in cold blood. The best thing we could do for him is make sure that he dies in the shootout.''

Maxwell started the engine and shifted into reverse. He backed out, shifted again and headed toward the exit. ''We find him, we give him a chance to surrender first.''

Gerber nodded. ''Sure, Jerry, that's exactly what we're going to do.''

''I mean it,'' said Maxwell.

''So do I,'' said Gerber.

They turned onto the main street, heading toward the Carasel Hotel, hoping that Reed, not knowing they had tumbled to him, would be sitting around waiting. And Gerber hoped that he would want to fight. He prayed he would.

15

CARASEL HOTEL, SAIGON

Reed sat naked on the bed, the water dripping from his body and soaking into the bedspread. He sat there for a long time, until the water had evaporated and he began to get cold in the icy blast of the air-conditioning. He stood up and wandered to the window, wondering what was happening to him. Nothing made sense anymore.

Then he remembered the dead girl in his bed at the other place, and he remembered Gerber's face staring at him across the table and knew that it was time to leave. Head over to the Cercle Raquette and hang around until he could make the necessary connection. Find the Vietcong and let them know that he was the one who had been feeding them the information. Let them know that he was burned and had to get out now. They'd help him because he'd helped them.

He dressed in his finest suit, a charcoal-colored silk, a single-breasted model that had been tailored by a shop that claimed a connection to the tailors of Hong Kong. It was a fine suit.

He put on a white shirt and a dark tie and then returned to the bathroom so that he could admire himself in the mirror.

Thi would have liked to see him in the suit. Hell, she would
have liked taking him out of it. Undressing him slowly, hanging up his clothes so they wouldn't wrinkle and then fucking
his brains out. As long as he let a little information drop
sometime during the visit.

As he'd done in the other room, he turned slowly, spotted
nothing that he wanted and walked into the main room. He
walked down the stairs until he reached the lobby. There were
a hundred people in it. GIs with Vietnamese women, officers
from all branches of the military, journalists, bellboys and
clerks. Lots of people who ignored him as he made his way
across the marble floor to the front door.

For a moment he stopped and looked out into the blazing
heat of noontime sun. It looked hot. People were sweating,
moving slowly to conserve their strength, and dodging into
doorways to escape the sun for a moment.

Reed pushed open the door as the doorman reached it. He
grinned at the man and gave him a five-dollar tip. Not pias-
ters, but a greenback. That would set him back on his heels.

He hailed a cab, never even thinking about the jeep that was
parked near the other hotel. He crawled into the back and
smelled the odor of other passengers. There was trash on the
floor. Candy wrappers and Coke cans and a condom that
looked to have been used, but not recently. Reed thought
about the shit getting on his shoes and then put the thought
out of his head.

"Where you go, Joe?"

Reed sat back and thought about that. He was beginning his
great escape in the back of an old cab with a Vietnamese driver
who could barely speak English.

"The Circle Racquet Club."

"What?"

"Cercle Raquette," said Reed, not sure that he had the
pronunciation right.

The driver nodded and entered the traffic. He turned once and went around the block so that he was heading in the opposite direction. It took them twenty minutes to get there, dodging through the traffic of Saigon's streets. The driver stopped on the street and Reed paid him.

The club was a massive structure that took up nearly the whole block. There was black wood and brass doors that opened into beautiful green lawns trimmed short and lined with carefully clipped hedges. Reed stood for a moment and then walked toward the French colonial-style clubhouse with its stucco walls and red tile roof.

He walked in, was stopped by a man in white who wanted to know if he was a member. The man spoke French.

"No," said Reed in English. "I might like to join, if that is possible."

The look on the man's face changed, as if he suddenly were forced to be gracious to a man he didn't like. In broken, heavily accented English, he said, "You follow me. I tour you."

Reed was shown the spacious locker room, the pool area and the tennis courts. A couple of women were playing, batting the balls over the net, but with no real instinct for the game. Playing at playing tennis.

They walked around the grounds, the gardens with their lush tropical plantings and bright flowers. The sun was bright and hot, and Reed felt the sweat beginning to soak his silk suit. Finally they returned to the pool and Reed sat down in a wicker chair.

"You mind if I relax for a moment?"

"You use bar. Drink. I return here, twenty minute."

"That would be nice," said Reed. As the man left, Reed settled in to watch the members of the Cercle Raquette, trying to figure out who might be VC. Who might be the contact he needed to make.

MAXWELL PULLED UP to the hotel, but there was no place to park. It was the first time that he had ever wanted to park in front of the place, and it was the first time that he had ever noticed that the street was lined with vehicles. He pulled in close, looped the chain through the steering wheel and hopped out.

Gerber climbed out the other side and then tilted the seat forward for Fetterman. As they came around the front of the jeep, a Vietnamese man came at them from the hotel.

"You no park there."

"I'm here on business," said Maxwell, trying to sound like a police officer.

"You no park."

Fetterman pushed past Maxwell and handed the man a five-dollar bill. "Watch the jeep for us, will you? We'll be back in ten minutes."

They entered the hotel and started for the stairs, then stopped. Maxwell walked over to the registration desk and asked for Reed's room key. The clerk thought nothing of it and handed it to him. Maxwell looked at the number, then showed it to Gerber.

They ran up the steps, the adrenaline beginning to pump, making it impossible to walk. In the jungle it was a high all the time. At any moment it could happen, or it might not. Probably wouldn't. But this was different. Gerber knew there would be shooting. Not necessarily him or Fetterman. They could take Reed without shooting, no matter how heavily armed he was. But there was still the edge, the excitement, knowing they were about to face an armed, dangerous, probably crazy man.

In the hallway they all slowed down as if one of them had ordered them to. Fetterman hurried ahead, taking a position on the far side of the door. Gerber leaned against the wall and Maxwell, the key extended, moved toward the knob. He stopped, pulled his pistol and then looked at the two Special Forces men.

Gerber nodded and drew the concealed Browning from his waistband. Fetterman produced his, holding it up against his shoulder, almost as if he were going to salute with it.

Maxwell nodded and knelt in front of the door, slowly inserting the key. If Reed was in there and had the safety chain on, or if he had bought a sliding bolt of his own, they wouldn't be able to surprise him.

Maxwell turned the key, felt the lock tumble, and reached up to the knob. He came to his feet and glanced right and left. Gerber and Fetterman were ready.

Without another moment's hesitation, Maxwell threw open the door and dived in. Gerber followed him, moving to the right side. He dropped to one knee, his pistol extended, pointing toward the bathroom door. Fetterman came in last, leaped over Maxwell and hit the floor, aiming into an empty corner of the room. If Reed had been anywhere in the room, he would have found himself facing a gun.

Maxwell jumped up and ran into the bathroom, hitting the wall, but finding it empty, too. He stepped out and holstered his weapon. "Clear."

Gerber got up and closed the door. Fetterman was on his feet smiling. "Took down the room in great shape, though."

"Yeah," said Gerber. "For what it was worth."

Maxwell went to the wardrobe and opened it. The clothes still hung in it. The bottom was littered with papers, boxes and extra shoes. He crouched in front of it and began to paw through its contents.

While he searched the papers, Gerber entered the bathroom. Reed's shaving gear was still there. A damp towel lay on the floor, and he felt the inside of the shower. Still damp, but in the humidity of Saigon, it was hard to tell how long it would take to dry.

He returned to the main room. "Looks like he hasn't checked out."

"No reason he should," said Maxwell.

"Bull," said Fetterman. "He's got to know we're on to him. Otherwise he'd still be over at MACV where we could find him."

Maxwell found a stack of papers and sat on the bed, thumbing through them.

"Now what?" asked Gerber.

"We've got to see if we can find a clue about where he'd go," said Maxwell.

Gerber moved to a pile of dirty clothes. He began searching through them, looking for anything that might have been left in the pockets.

Fetterman walked to the window and looked out, but there was nothing to see except an alley piled with trash and one old Chevy that didn't look as if it ran.

Maxwell threw the papers on the floor. "Nothing here." He turned and jerked open the drawer of the nightstand. Nothing in there but a well-thumbed *Penthouse*. He rubbed his chin with his hand.

"Shit," was all he said.

It was then that Gerber found the key. "Hello," he said as he pulled it from the pocket. "Look what we have here."

Maxwell rolled across the bed and took the key, turning over the tag where he could almost make out the name of the hotel. He walked to the window and held it up in the light.

"I know this place," said Maxwell. "Sleazy hotbed number. Wonder why he has a key?"

"Let's go look at it," said Gerber.

REED FINISHED HIS DRINK and his escort returned. He smiled down at Reed and asked, "You have seen too much?"

It took Reed a moment to decipher that and then grinned. "It is a very beautiful club."

"You will join?"

Reed took a deep breath and looked up at the man. "Do you get many soldiers in here?"

"No. American soldiers fight war."

Reed realized there was absolutely no way to ask the man if the Vietcong were represented. He knew that at Vung Tau, a coastal city known for its beaches, the Americans, South Vietnamese and the Vietcong shared the facility, each group pretending that the other didn't exist.

There was only one thing to do. Either join the club so that he could hang around longer or get the hell out. If he did that, there was no place for him to go. The airlines were all booked weeks in advance, and the airline would check with the embassy to make sure he was authorized to fly out of the country. He needed help escaping.

He set his empty glass on the wicker table near him and then stood. "Let us fill out an application, and then I shall pay for a year's membership."

The man's English suddenly improved. He said, "Very good, sir."

Reed followed the man through the rich hallways with their fine woods and subdued lighting. It was an elegance that was in stark contrast to the hotel where the dead Vietnamese woman waited for him. Sleaze next to splendor. Foreigners having the money, the power and the connections for the finer things that Vietnam had to offer, while the people lived in poverty, begging for money to survive. It all meant that he was right in the course he had taken. Someone had to show them the errors of their ways.

THEY SPOTTED THE JEEP parked near the hotel as they drove up. Maxwell pulled up close and said, "We could stake it out and take him on the street."

"No," said Gerber. "We're better off taking him in his room if we can. There's less chance of something going wrong that way."

"And no prying eyes to watch," added Fetterman.

Maxwell crept forward and parked his jeep near the other. Fetterman leaped out and opened the hood of Reed's, taking the distributor to disable it.

"At least he won't use this to escape," he said.

They made their way to the hotel, saw that no one was watching the lobby, and walked up the stairs. But this time the excitement was missing. They had thought they had him once and had missed. Even with the jeep parked on the street, they weren't sure that he was going to be there.

At the door they took up their positions as Maxwell tried the key. It worked easily. He threw open the door and dived in, just as he had before.

This time neither Gerber nor Fetterman followed. They covered from the hall, but before they had moved, they had spotted the body in the bed. They knew that Reed wouldn't be there.

Gerber entered quickly, waited for Fetterman and then closed the door.

"Jesus, he did it again," said Maxwell.

Fetterman moved forward and reached for a pulse, knowing there wouldn't be one. The waxy hard look of the skin, and the smell of bowel, told him the woman was dead. Still he had to check.

Maxwell rubbed his face with his hand and then stroked the back of his head. "Jesus."

"Okay," said Gerber. "I think we can now assume that he's on the run. You don't leave the body in your room unless you're not coming back."

Maxwell turned and stared at the body. Fetterman jerked the top sheet from the bed and covered the dead woman with it. As soon as he could no longer see her, Maxwell looked at Gerber.

"How can he keep doing it?"

"There are people like that. They get a taste of it and you can't stop them. Want to kill everything in sight. Sometimes you channel the tendency by giving them special assignments, if they can control themselves most of the time. If not, you get rid of them. Get them help. Reed's beyond that. He likes it too much.''

"How do you know?''

"Because he used his knife again. Shoved it in and watched her die. No reason to kill this woman. The other one, yes. She could finger him, but he did this one because he wanted to do it again.''

"Jesus, we've got to stop him.''

"Now you understand,'' said Fetterman.

"But where do we look now? You say he's running. Where would he go?''

"Running in Vietnam is different than running in the World. Here, you can't just drive out into the country. Someone might shoot your ass off. You can't get on an airplane to fly out. You could get lost in the underground of Saigon, but I don't think our boy would last long there.''

"Why not?''

"Because they don't appreciate someone killing off their people for no reason.''

Fetterman broke into the discussion. "What are we going to do about this?''

"Give the MPs a shout and let them take over,'' said Gerber. "Give them a description of Reed and let them know what he's done. They might finish the job for us.''

"No, sir,'' said Fetterman. "This is one guy I want to get myself. I want him real bad, now.''

"Let's see what he's left behind,'' said Gerber.

They searched the room, but there was even less of Reed in it than there had been in the other. Almost nothing, and yet the body of the woman told them more than any of them wanted to know about it. A ruthless man who killed on a whim.

Then, when it looked like there was nothing else to do, Fetterman found the letter. An unaddressed envelope that he thought nothing about until he opened it and read the contents.

"Here it is," he said.

Gerber moved over so that he could read over the master sergeant's shoulder. "Jesus."

"Lays it out here, doesn't he?" said Fetterman.

"Confession is good for the soul," said Gerber, "but to write all this down . . ."

"He was going to mail it to this Thom guy," said Fetterman. "Maybe we should alert the FBI about him. Let them keep an eye on him."

"Jerry?"

"I'll take care of it."

"We'd better hang on to this letter," said Gerber. He glanced at Maxwell. "Well, if you had any doubts, this should take care of them all."

"Came over here with the idea in mind. Going to undercut us by supplying information to the enemy. Shit. And we did a background check on him. Came up clean."

"Unless he'd done something that the police would have recorded, or unless someone had something bad to say, it would be clean."

Fetterman flipped the pages and read the last one. He held it up for Gerber to see.

"Makes sense," said Gerber.

"What?"

"He headed over to the Cercle Raquette." Gerber looked at Maxwell. "You know anything about the place?"

"Old French club that was forced to allow Americans and anyone else with the price of admission in. Not enough French left here for the upkeep. Reed's right about one thing, we suspect that top VC officials, along with some of the top South Vietnamese officials, belong. Club tolerates the VC because they won't throw a satchel charge over the wall. Has to tolerate the South Vietnamese so they can pretend they don't know who the VC are.''

"Then that's where we need to go next," said Fetterman. "No reason not to."

"Except that it was pretty stupid to leave the letter lying around," said Maxwell.

"Unless he's crazy," Fetterman suggested.

"There is that," agreed Gerber.

16

THE CERCLE RAQUETTE CLUB

Maxwell stopped on the street, outside the black wood and brass doors of the wall that marked the perimeter of the club. He looked at Gerber and Fetterman. "How do we do this?"

Gerber took a deep breath and glanced at the club facade. "Head in, look around, and if we see him, convince him to come with us."

Maxwell sat hunched over the wheel, both hands on it. He was staring down at the floorboards. "What if he refuses? The man is crazy."

"Jerry, there's no way we can cover all the bases. We suspect the man is in there. Maybe we can walk up right behind him and say let's go to MACV. Maybe he's crazy and will draw down on us. Maybe he'll run."

"So what do you do?"

"Jerry, he's an untrained civilian. Even if he is armed, Sergeant Fetterman and I can take him. That's exactly what we'll do, and if he dies in the attempt, that's his problem. We've now got that body in the old hotel. Nothing's going to come back at us."

Maxwell glanced to the right. "Then let's do it."

"This time let's spread out," said Fetterman. "That way if he breaks, one of us should be in a position to cut him off."

"Good," said Gerber.

"One question," said Fetterman. "Just what are the rules of engagement?"

"Return fire for fire received. No, let me modify that. You see a gun in his hand, drop the hammer on him."

"Yes, sir."

Maxwell didn't move. "Anyone hears that, they're going to call it premeditation."

"No one here but us friends."

"Good point," said Maxwell.

Gerber got out of the jeep and moved across the sidewalk. When Fetterman and Maxwell joined him, he entered the club grounds. For a moment they stood in the shadows and took in the scene. The manicured lawns, trimmed hedges and the buildings of the clubhouses and the tennis courts. A beautiful place.

"Heading to the right," said Fetterman.

Maxwell nodded. "I'll go left."

"That leaves me straight ahead. Let's meet back here in forty-five minutes."

"Yes, sir," said Fetterman.

Gerber started across the lawn and was intercepted by a short man in white. He fell into step with Gerber, looking as if he were trying to figure out what to say. Finally he asked, "You guest?"

"Looking for a friend."

"You tell me and I tell you."

"He'd be a new member, you might not know who he is." Gerber glanced at the man.

"You tell me."

Gerber stopped and looked down at the man. "His name's Reed. An American."

"You look by the pool."

"What?" Gerber turned to look at the clubhouse.

"You go there," said the man, pointing. "Around to pool. You look there."

Gerber took a dollar in MPC from his pocket and handed it to the Vietnamese man. "Thank you."

The man took the tip and slipped away, disappearing into the plantings. Gerber headed toward the pool, finding it around the corner. He looked at the wicker furniture around it. There were a few people sitting in the sun. Men and women, none of them Vietnamese, with one exception, and she wasn't full-blooded. A tall thin woman in a bikini walked to the diving board.

Gerber spotted Reed sitting in a wicker chair, holding a drink in his left hand. Unfortunately the man was looking right at him. There was no way for Gerber to hide. He thought about waving as if they were old friends and decided against it. He wasn't going to call attention to himself if he could help it.

He turned and headed toward the man. Reed took a deep drink from the glass in his hand and then slowly set it on the wicker table next to him. He stood and stretched, and then as casually as possible, began walking in the other direction.

Gerber kept moving toward him slowly. The man glanced over his shoulder and took off running, bumping into a Vietnamese carrying a tray of glasses. The Vietnamese bounced off and fell to the grass.

Gerber hurried in pursuit. He caught a glimpse of Reed running across a patch of lawn, angling toward a door. Gerber followed. He hit the door and saw a narrow carpeted hallway. A door at the far end was just closing.

Gerber ran down the hall and pushed on the door. There was a single shot. A loud bang and a piece of wood near his shoulder splintered. Gerber ducked, his back against the wall, and saw there was no one in the corridor with him.

Again he pushed the door. This time nothing happened. He stood up, flattened against the wall and eased the door open.

The room was dark but seemed to be empty. Gerber reached around and touched his pistol, still tucked into his waistband.

He entered the room, stepping away from the door. There was a single window, the curtains drawn. At the other side was another door. Gerber ran to it, punched it and dropped back. Reed, if he was on the other side, didn't fire.

Gerber slammed into the door then and dodged away from it. He found himself in another corridor. He started down it, glancing right and left. He grabbed the door knobs as he went by them, trying each one, but everything seemed to be locked. He reached the end of the corridor but didn't see the man anywhere. Somehow Reed had avoided him.

He stood there for a moment. Fetterman appeared in the doorway and came toward him.

"Had him," said Gerber, "but he got away."

"Fired a shot?"

"Tore up the woodwork but missed me. He didn't say a word, just took off running." Gerber touched his forehead with the sleeve of his jungle fatigues.

Then from outside there was a scream, a shot and then another scream. Gerber ran toward the door with Fetterman right behind him.

"Over there?"

"Yes, sir."

They both took off in that direction. There was more screaming, and a woman in a bikini ran by them. Her face was a mask of terror.

They raced around one planting and Gerber slid to a halt. Reed was on the other side of the pool, waving a pistol. He pointed it at a Vietnamese waiter and fired. The man spun to the ground, blood leaking from his chest.

Gerber reached up under his jungle jacket and drew his pistol. He pointed to Fetterman and then off to the right. Fetterman understood immediately. He drew his own weapon and took off, crouched over, using the plantings for cover.

Gerber ran the other way, leaping toward the dirt and rolling toward a planter. Reed fired a shot and Gerber heard it snap past him.

"On the right," yelled Fetterman.

"Got you."

Reed heard that, looking from where Gerber had dived to cover and where Fetterman's voice had come. He fired again and again, first at one and then at the other.

Then he turned and ran again. Gerber popped up, one knee on the soft wet grass. Holding his pistol in both hands, he aimed at Reed. The sights were centered in the middle of the man's back. He squeezed the trigger, but as the weapon fired, Reed jumped and then rolled over.

Fetterman appeared at the far end of the plantings on the other side of the pool. He was angling toward Reed. He had his pistol out, but wasn't aiming it.

Reed was up and running again. He rounded a corner, disappearing from sight. While Fetterman chased him, Gerber tried to cut him off. He ran into the building, down a hallway, toward the rear of it. He found a window and looked out. Reed was running across the tennis courts. They were deserted. A racquet lay among several abandoned balls.

Gerber opened the window and jumped out. He was up and running then. Fetterman no longer had the angle on him. Gerber did.

Reed stopped and whirled. He fired at Gerber. Two quick shots. One of them shattered the window. Gerber snapped off another shot but missed. Fetterman kept running right at him.

Reed fired once at Fetterman and then took off again. He ran into a building. Gerber raced after him. He and Fetterman reached the door at the same time. Gerber grabbed the handle and when Fetterman nodded, he jerked it open.

The master sergeant dived through but there was no shooting. Gerber leaped in, saw another door and ran to it. As they reached it there was a burst of firing. Three quick shots, a pause and then half a dozen more. Two men firing at one another as fast as they could pull the triggers.

Gerber opened the door and leaped in. He rolled over, landing on his belly, his weapon extended in front of him, pointing at the body on the floor. Reed was lying in a pool of blood.

Slowly Gerber got to his feet. Fetterman joined him, his pistol pointing at Reed's head. They advanced on him. Fetterman stepped on his hand and pulled the pistol from it. He glanced at Gerber.

"Man's dead."

There was a wail of sirens.

"Maybe we'd better split," said Fetterman.

"Too late now." He turned and looked at the door. Maxwell stood there, looking down at the body. His pistol was held in his right hand. His face was pasty white.

"You okay, Jerry?"

Maxwell didn't respond. He took a step forward and then stopped. He stared at Reed's face, as white as his own.

"Jerry, you okay?" Gerber asked again.

"Never shot anyone I knew. Never watched them open their eyes wide as they realized they were dead. Never."

"Jerry, you better snap out of it."

"Never."

"Jerry, there are cops on the way. You're going have to get it together. Tell them what's going on."

"Layons. Tell them to call Captain John Layons, 716th MP Battalion."

Gerber turned to Fetterman. "Get Maxwell out of here. I'll meet with the cops and tell them what's going on."

"I can stay, sir."

"No, get out. Get him to the jeep. You get clear, call the embassy and get the ambassador or someone over here."

"Yes, sir."

Fetterman moved toward Maxwell and pried the gun from his stiff fingers. "Jerry, let's go."

Fetterman guided Maxwell out the door.

The sirens were closer now. Gerber figured the police would be slowed by the panicked civilians. He tucked his pistol under his fatigue jacket and moved to the door. He opened it and saw a number of MPs and White Mice running across the neat lawn. Two of them broke off, heading toward the back of the building. He hoped Fetterman had gotten Maxwell out of there, but figured it didn't matter that much.

Two MPs with M-16s burst through the door. They saw Reed's body and then Gerber, swinging toward him. One of them kept Gerber covered as the other advanced.

Gerber held his hands out in plain sight. "I'm MacKenzie K. Gerber, Captain, Special Forces."

The MP with the rifle asked, "You shoot this man?"

"No, I didn't. But I know who did. Before we get too far in this, you'd better call Captain Layons."

"He's on the way," said the MP.

"Then we've got no problem."

IT WAS TWO DAYS later. Gerber and Fetterman were eating lunch at the Carasel Hotel. Morrow had joined them late and she had brought Maxwell with her. He still looked slightly sick.

"Sit down, Jerry."

Maxwell dropped into the chair, nodded at Fetterman and then reached over, taking Gerber's beer away from him. He tilted it to his lips and drained most of it.

"The big boys are royally hosed about this," said Maxwell. "They don't know what to do. Reed was a traitor, selling information to the VC. He was a killer, having stabbed two, maybe more Saigon prostitutes . . ."

"What does that mean?" asked Morrow.

"Not for attribution, Robin," said Maxwell, "but I think the White Mice and the MPs used Reed to clear a few cases off the books. Made everyone look good."

"Then why are people pissed?" asked Fetterman.

"Get real, Tony. A gunfight in the exclusive Cercle Raquette. Diplomats running for their lives. There have been a few memos passed from one embassy to another."

"But it means nothing, right?" asked Gerber.

"When all is said and done, we're all heroes. Stopped a deranged killer. Everyone would like to sweep the episode under the rug. The news stories have run their course."

Fetterman stopped eating and sat back in his chair. "That's probably best. Forget about it. We plugged the leak and Reed didn't survive the plumbing operation. Everyone's happy."

Gerber felt dissatisfied, though. Something was missing. He had a sense that they had accomplished nothing. Everyone had blundered around until they had tripped over the leak. He'd then freaked out and died in a gunfight. He'd killed other people, been responsible for the deaths of more and had died himself. But not satisfactorily.

"You have a problem, Mack?" asked Morrow.

It struck him finally what it was. "Yeah, I do. We've an American citizen, giving aid and comfort to the enemy. We've got a man leaking top-secret information to the VC, and everyone is upset because he died in a gunfight at the Cercle Raquette. No one seems to care what the man had been doing. That his spying might have lengthened the war and that it certainly compromised some of our efforts."

"It wasn't that big a deal," said Morrow.

"But damn it, Robin, it was. Anytime you help the enemy, no matter how you do it, it's treason."

"Some people don't think this war should be fought."

Gerber didn't want to get into a political discussion with her about it, but said, "Makes no difference at this point. We're in it."

Fetterman saw the direction the conversation was taking and interrupted it. "I think we should be grateful that we managed to get it stopped."

Gerber, the anger blazing, looked at Fetterman and then back to Morrow. Finally he said, "That's right. Let's just be happy it's over."

"All right," said Morrow. "Now, if you're finished eating, I have the afternoon off."

"Then I'm finished." He stood up. "Tony, I don't want to see or hear from you until tomorrow."

"Yes, sir."

Gerber waited for Morrow to stand up, and then together they left the restaurant. As they disappeared through the door, Fetterman looked at Maxwell. "We might as well get drunk."

"Might as well."

Fetterman raised a hand and then ordered the first round.

HALF A WORLD AWAY, Thom sat in the basement office and read the short news story again. A man had been killed in some kind of terrorist act at a posh Saigon racquet club. There weren't many details other than the name of the victim and a statement from the ambassador who said that it was a tragic event. The civilians in Saigon were in as much danger from the Vietcong terrorists as were the soldiers in the field.

Thom knew better than that. He knew what his friend, Philip Reed, had been doing, and was sure he had been killed by the CIA because he was spying on the Americans. Trying to end that rotten war with positive action.

Thom felt tears sting his eyes as he stood up and walked to the windows that had been covered in newspaper. "God damn it, Phil, what in the hell did you get yourself into?"

He wadded up the paper and threw it, but it loosened and fell to the floor. He kicked at a table, flipping it, and hurt his toe.

"Why?" he asked, never realizing that it was the same question that was on the lips of the men as they had died in the ambush.

GLOSSARY

AC—Aircraft commander. The pilot in charge of the aircraft.

ADO—A-Detachment's area of operations.

AFVN—Armed Forces radio and television network in Vietnam. Army PFC Pat Sajak was probably the most memorable of AFVN's DJs with his loud and long, "GOOOOOOOOOOOOD MORNing, Vietnam." The spinning Wheel of Fortune gives no clues about his whereabouts today.

AGGRESSOR FATIGUES—Black fatigues called aggressor fatigues because they are the color of the uniforms worn by the aggressors during war games in the World during training.

AIT—Advanced Individual Training. The school soldiers were sent to after Basic.

AK-47—Assault rifle normally used by the North Vietnamese and the Vietcong.

ANGRY-109—AN-109—The radio used by the Special Forces for long-range communications.

AO—Area of Operations.

AO DAI—Long, dresslike garment, split up the sides and worn over pants.

AP—Air Police. The old designation for the guards on Air Force bases. Now referred to as security police.

AP ROUNDS—Armor-piercing ammunition.

APU—Auxiliary Power Unit. An outside source of power used to start aircraft engines.

ARC LIGHT—Term used for a B-52 bombing mission. Also known as heavy arty.

ARVN—Army of the Republic of Vietnam. A South Vietnamese soldier. Also known as Marvin Arvin.

ASA—Army Security Agency.

ASH AND TRASH—Refers to helicopter support missions that did not involve a direct combat role. They were hauling supplies, equipment, mail and all sorts of ash and trash.

AST—Control officer between the men in isolation and the outside world. He is responsible for taking care of all the problems.

AUTOVON—Army phone system that allows soldiers on base to call another base, bypassing the civilian phone system.

BDA—Bomb Damage Assessment. The official report on how well the bombing mission went.

BIG RED ONE—Nickname of the First Infantry Division. It came from the shoulder patch that contains a big, red numeral one.

BISCUIT—C-rations.

BODY COUNT—Number of enemy killed, wounded or captured during an operation. Used by Saigon and Washington as a means of measuring progress of the war.

BOOM-BOOM—Term used by the Vietnamese prostitutes in selling their product.

BOONDOGGLE—Any military operation that hasn't been completely thought out. An operation that is ridiculous.

BOONIE HATS—Soft cap worn by the grunt in the field when he wasn't wearing his steel pot.

BROWNING M-2—The 50-caliber machine gun manufactured by Browning.

BROWNING M-35—The automatic pistol, a 9 mm weapon, that became the favorite of the Special Forces.

BUSHMASTER—Jungle warfare expert or soldier skilled in jungle navigation. Also a large deadly snake not common to Vietnam but mighty tasty.

C AND C—Command Control aircraft that circled overhead to direct the combined air and ground operations.

CAO BOIS—(cowboys) Term that referred to the criminals of Saigon who rode motorcycles.

CARIBOU—Cargo transport plane.

CHICOM—Chinese Communist. Troops or weapons and equipment supplied by Red China.

CHINOOK—Army Aviation twin-engine helicopter. A CH-47. Also known as a SHIT HOOK.

CHOCK—Refers to the number of the aircraft in the flight. Chock Three is the third, Chock Six is the sixth.

CLAYMORE—Antipersonnel mine that fires seven hundred and fifty steel balls with a lethal range of fifty meters.

CLOSE AIR SUPPORT—Use of airplanes and helicopters to fire on enemy units near friendly troops.

CO CONG—Female Vietcong.

COLT—Soviet-built small transport plane. The NATO code name for Soviet and Warsaw Pact transport planes all begin with the letter C.

COMSEC—Communications security.

CONEX—Steel container about ten feet high, ten feet deep and ten feet long used to haul equipment and supplies.

CS—A persistent form of improved tear gas (usually dispersed as a fine powder from grenades) used as a military and riot control agent.

DAC CONG—Sappers who attack in the front ranks to blow up the wire so that the infantry can assault the camp.

DAI UY—Vietnamese army rank, the equivalent of captain.

DEROS—Date of estimated return from overseas.

DIRNSA—Director, National Security Agency.

E AND E—Escape and Evasion.

FEET WET—Term used by pilots to describe flight over water.

FIELD GRADE—Refers to officers above the rank of captain but under that of brigadier general. In other words, majors, lieutenant colonels and colonels.

FIRECRACKER—Special artillery shell that explodes into a number of small bomblets to detonate later. It is the artillery version of the cluster bomb and was a secret weapon employed tactically for the first time at Khe Sanh.

FIRST SHIRT—First Sergeant.

FIVE—Radio call sign for the executive officer of a unit.

FNG—Fucking new guy.

FOB—Forward operating base.

FOX MIKE—FM radio.

FREEDOM BIRD—Name given to any aircraft that took troops out of Vietnam. Usually referred to the commercial jet flights that took men back to the World.

GARAND—The M-1 rifle that was replaced by the M-14. Issued to the Vietnamese early in the war.

GO-TO-HELL RAG—Towel or any large cloth worn around the neck by grunts.

GRAIL—NATO name for the shoulder-fired SA-7 surface-to-air missile.

GUARD THE RADIO—Stand by in the commo bunker and listen for messages.

GUIDELINE—NATO name for the SA-2 surface-to-air missile.

GUNSHIP—Armed helicopter or cargo plane that carries weapons instead of cargo.

HE—High-explosive ammunition.

HOOTCH—Almost any shelter, from temporary to long-term.

HORN—Term referring to a specific kind of radio operations that used satellites to rebroadcast the messages.

HORSE—See BISCUIT.

HOTEL THREE—Helicopter landing area at Saigon's Tan Son Nhut Airport.

HUEY—UH-1 helicopter.

HUMINT—Human Intelligence resource. In other words, they talked to someone who gave them the information.

ICS—Official name of the intercom system in an aircraft.

IN-COUNTRY—Term used to refer to American troops operating in South Vietnam. They were all in-country.

INTELLIGENCE—Any information about enemy operations. It can include troop movements, weapons capabilities, biographies of enemy commanders and general information about terrain features. Any information that would be useful in planning a mission.

KA-BAR—Type of military combat knife.

KIA—Killed in action. (Since the US was not engaged in a declared war, the use of the term KIA was not authorized. KIA came to mean enemy dead. Americans were KHA—killed in hostile action).

KLICK—A thousand meters. A kilometer.

LIMA LIMA—Land line. Refers to telephone communications between two points on the ground.

LLDB—Luc Luong Dac Biet. The South Vietnamese Special Forces. Sometimes referred to as the Look Long, Duck Back.

LP—Listening Post. A position outside the perimeter manned by a couple of soldiers to give advance warning of enemy activity.

LRRP—Long-range Reconnaissance Patrol.

LSA—Lubricant used by soldiers on their weapons to ensure they will continue to operate properly.

LZ—Landing zone.

M-3A1—Also known as a grease gun. A .45-caliber submachine gun favored in World War Two by the GIs because its slow rate of fire meant that the barrel didn't rise and they didn't burn through their ammo as fast as they did with some other weapons.

M-14—Standard rifle of the U.S. Army, eventually replaced by the M-16. It fired the standard NATO round—7.62 mm.

M-16—Standard infantry weapon of the Vietnam War. It fired the 5.56 mm ammunition.

M-79—Short-barrel shoulder-fired weapon that fires a 40 mm grenade. These can be high explosives, white phosphorus or canister.

M-113—Numerical designation of an armored personnel carrier.

MACV—Military Assistance Command, Vietnam, replaced MAAG in 1964.

MAD MINUTE—A specified time on a base camp when the men in the bunkers would clear their weapons. It came to mean the random firing of all the camp's weapons just as fast as everyone could shoot.

MATCU—Marine Air Traffic Control Unit.

MEDEVAC—Also called Dustoff. Helicopter used to take the wounded to medical facilities.

MI—Military intelligence.

MIA—Missing in action.

MONOPOLY MONEY—A term used by the servicemen in Vietnam to describe the MPC handed out in lieu of regular U.S. currency.

MOS—Military Occupation Speciality. It is a job description.

MPC—Military Payment Certificates. The monopoly money used instead of real cash.

NCO—A noncommissioned officer. A noncom. A sergeant.

NCOIC—NCO in charge. The senior NCO in a unit, detachment or patrol.

NDB—Nondirectional beacon. A radio beacon that can be used for homing.

NEXT—The man who was the next to be rotated home. See SHORT.

NINETEEN—The average age of the combat soldier in Vietnam, as opposed to twenty-six in World War II.

NOUC MAM—A foul-smelling sauce used by the Vietnamese.

NVA—The North Vietnamese Army. Also used to designate a soldier from North Vietnam.

ONTOS—A Marine weapon that consists of six 106 mm recoilless rifles mounted on a tracked vehicle.

ORDER OF BATTLE—A listing of the units available and to be used during the battle. It is not necessarily a list of how or when the units will be used, but a listing of who and what could be used.

P (PIASTER)—The basic monetary unit in South Vietnam, worth slightly less than a penny.

PETA-PRIME—Tarlike substance that melted in the heat of the day to become a sticky black nightmare that clung to boots, clothes and equipment. It was used to hold down the dust during the dry season.

PETER PILOT—The copilot in a helicopter.

PLF—Parachute landing fall. The roll used by parachutists on landing.

POL—Petroleum, oil and lubricants. The refueling point on many military bases.

POW—Prisoner of war.

PRC-10—Portable radio.

PRC-25—A lighter portable radio that replaced the PRC-10.

PULL PITCH—Term used by helicopter pilots that means they are going to take off.

PUNJI STAKE—Sharpened bamboo hidden to penetrate the foot, sometimes dipped in feces.

PUZZLE PALACE—A term referring to the Pentagon. It was called the puzzle palace because no one knew what was going on in it. The Puzzle Palace East referred to MACV or USARV Headquarters in Saigon.

RED LEGS—A term that refers to the artillerymen. It comes from the old Army where the artillerymen wore a red stripe on the legs of their uniforms.

REMF—A rear-echelon motherfucker.

RINGKNOCKER—Graduate of a military academy. The term refers to the ring worn by all graduates.

RON—Remain Overnight. Term used by flight crews to indicate a flight that would last longer than a day.

RPD—Soviet-made light machine gun, 7.62 mm.

RTO—Radio telephone operator. The radio man of a unit.

RUFF-PUFFS—A term applied to the RF-PFs, the regional forces and popular forces. Militia drawn from the local population.

S-3—The company-level operations officer. He is the same as the G-3 on a general's staff.

SA-2—A surface-to-air missile fired from a fixed site. It is a radar-guided missile nearly thirty-five feet long.

SA-7—A surface-to-air missile that is shoulder-fired and infrared homing.

SACSA—Special Assistant for Counterinsurgency and Special Activities.

SAFE AREA—Selected area for evasion. It doesn't mean that the area is safe from the enemy, only that the terrain, location or local population make the area a good place for escape and evasion.

SAM TWO—A reference to the SA-2 Guideline.

SAR—Search and rescue. SAR forces are the people involved in search and rescue missions.

SECDEF—Secretary of Defense.

SHORT-TIME—A GI term for a quickie.

SHORT-TIMER—Person who had been in Vietnam for nearly a year and who would be rotated back to the World soon. When his DEROS was the shortest in the unit, the person was said to be next.

SINGLE DIGIT MIDGET—A soldier with fewer than ten days left in-country.

SIX—Radio call sign for the unit commander.

SKS—Soviet-made carbine.

SMG—Submachine gun.

SOG—Studies and Observations Group. Cover name used for MACV Special Operations.

SOI—Signal operating instructions. The booklet that contained the call signs and radio frequencies of the units in Vietnam.

SOP—Standard operating procedure.

SPIKE TEAM—Special Forces team made up for a direct action mission.

STEEL POT—The standard U.S. Army helmet. The steel pot was the outer metal cover.

TAOR—Tactical area of operational responsibility.

TEAM UNIFORM OR COMPANY UNIFORM—UHF radio frequency on which the team or the company communicates. Frequencies were changed periodically in an attempt to confuse the enemy.

THE WORLD—The United States.

THREE—Radio call sign of the operations officer.

THREE CORPS—The military area around Saigon. Vietnam was divided into four corps areas.

TOC—Tactical operations center.

TO&E—Table of organization and equipment. A detailed listing of all the men and equipment assigned to a unit.

TOT—Time over target. It refers to the time that the aircraft are supposed to be over the drop zone with the parachutists, or the target if the planes are bombers.

TRICK CHIEF—NCOIC for a shift.

TRIPLE A—Antiaircraft Artillery or AAA. Anything used to shoot at airplanes and helicopters.

TWO—Radio call sign of the Intelligence officer.

TWO-OH-ONE (201) FILE—The military records file that listed all a soldier's qualifications, training, experience and abilities. It was passed from unit to unit so that the new commander would have some idea about the capabilities of the incoming soldier.

UMZ—Ultramilitarized zone, the name GIs gave to the DMZ (DeMilitarized Zone).

UNIFORM—Refers to UHF radio. Company Uniform would be the frequency assigned to that company.

URC-10—A small emergency communications radio used by Special Forces LRRPs.

USARV—United States Army, Vietnam.

VC—Vietcong, called Victor Charlie (phonetic alphabet) or just Charlie.

VIETCONG—A contraction of Vietnam Cong San (Vietnamese Communist).

VIET CONG SAN—The Vietnamese Communists. A term in use since 1956.

WHITE MICE—Refers to the South Vietnamese military police because they all wore white helmets.

WIA—Wounded in action.

WILLIE PETE—WP, white phosphorus, called smoke rounds. Also used as antipersonnel weapons.

WSO—Weapons system officer. The name given to the man who rode in the back seat of a Phantom because he was responsible for the weapons systems.

XO—Executive officer of a unit.

X-RAY—A term that refers to an engineer assigned to a unit.

ZAP—To ding, pop caps or shoot. To kill.

"Able Team will go anywhere, do anything, in order to complete their mission."
—*West Coast Review of Books*

SUPER ABLE TEAM #1
DICK STIVERS

The Desmondos, an organized street gang, terrorize the streets of Los Angeles armed with AK-47s and full-auto Uzis.

Carl Lyons and his men are sent in to follow the trail of blood and drugs to the power behind these teenage terrorists.

The Desmondos are bad, but they haven't met Able Team.

Trouble erupts for Nile Barrabas and his men when an undersea Soviet war base pits them against their most deadly enemy.

THE BARRABAS WAR

JACK HILD

A full-scale war is about to break out when suspected acts of Turkish terrorism result in furious Greek retaliation. Barrabas and his elite mercenaries discover a state-of-the-art command station and a sinister Soviet plot lurking beneath the Aegean Sea!

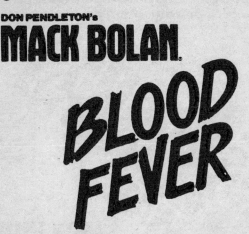

The line between good and evil is a tightrope no man should walk. Unless that man is the Executioner.

BLOWOUT $3.95 ☐
Framed for murder and wanted by both sides of the law, Bolan escapes into the icy German underground to stalk a Mafia-protected drug baron.

TIGHTROPE $3.95 ☐
When top officials of international intelligence agencies are murdered, Mack Bolan pits his skill against an alliance of renegade agents and uncovers a deadly scheme to murder the U.S. President.

MOVING TARGET $3.95 ☐
America's most powerful corporations are reaping huge profits by dealing in arms with anyone who can pay the price. Dogged by assassins, Mack Bolan becomes caught in a power struggle that might be his last.

FLESH & BLOOD $3.95 ☐
When Asian communities are victimized by predators among their own—thriving gangs of smugglers, extortionists and pimps—they turn to Mack Bolan for help.

Total Amount	$	_____
Plus 75¢ Postage		.75
Payment enclosed	$	_____

Vietnam: Ground Zero is written by men who saw it all, did it all and lived to tell it all

"Some of the most riveting war fiction written..."
—Ed Gorman, *Cedar Rapids Gazette*

STRIKE $3.95 ☐
An elite Special Forces team is dispatched when heavy traffic in enemy supplies to Nui Ba Den has Intelligence in Saigon worried. Primed for action, Mack Gerber and his men wage a firefight deep inside a mountain fortress, while the VC outside are poised for a suicide raid against an American political delegation.

SHIFTING FIRES $3.95 ☐
An American Special Forces squad is assembled to terminate a renowned general suspected of directing operations at the siege of Khe Sanh, where six thousand U.S. troops are pinned down by NVA regulars.

THE RAID $3.95 ☐
The Pentagon calls in experts in unconventional warfare when a Soviet training contingent is discovered in North Vietnam. Their mission: attack and kill every Russian in the place... and get out alive.

Total Amount	$ _____
Plus 75¢ Postage	.75
Payment enclosed	$ _____

Please send a check or money order payable to Gold Eagle Books.

In the U.S.	In Canada
Gold Eagle Books	Gold Eagle Books
901 Fuhrmann Blvd.	P.O. Box 609
Box 1325	Fort Erie, Ontario
Buffalo, NY 14269-1325	L2A 5X3

Please Print
Name: _____
Address: _____
City: _____
State/Prov: _____
Zip/Postal Code: _____

GOLD EAGLE

SV:GZ-A